No one would leave a baby alone in the woods—would they?

Cautiously, Katie walked through the birch trees, looking around on all sides. The awful shrieking grew louder. Katie was definitely getting closer, but closer to what?

As she neared a mossy boulder between two ancient birch trees, Katie froze. Whatever was making the noise was behind the boulder.

Katie flattened herself against the boulder and carefully peered over the top. "Oh!" she cried in surprise.

A red-faced baby in a pink romper sat propped against the other side of the boulder, screaming wildly.

There was no sign of anyone else at all.

The Baby Angel

FOREVER ANGELS

The Baby Angel

Suzanne Weyn

Rainbow Bridge®

Troll

Text copyright © 1995 by Chardiet Unlimited, Inc., and Suzanne Weyn.
Cover illustration copyright © 1995 by Mark English.
Cover border photography by Katrina.
Angel stickers (#5500-0018) copyright © 1994 by Gallery Graphics, Inc., Noel, MO, 64854. Used with permission.

Published by Rainbow Bridge, an imprint and trademark of Troll Communications L.L.C.

Printed in the United States of America.

10 9 8 7 6 5 4 3 2

Dedicated to Tisha Hamilton with deep thanks
for all her creative contributions, story ideas,
and strong commitment to this series.
You're an angel.

The Baby Angel

1

"Hot dog! Hot diggety dog!"

Katie rolled her eyes and laughed quietly at the exuberant yells coming from the kitchen. Aunt Rainie's voice sounded so high-pitched and excited, it was almost hard to believe the noise was human. She was really wild about something this afternoon.

Her eyes still twinkling with merriment, Katie glanced across the green velveteen living room couch. Her twenty-year-old cousin Mel sat at the other end, intently watching a motorcycle race on TV. Did he think it was funny, too? Whenever something struck her funny, Katie always liked to share the joke with someone else.

Mel didn't even look up. Absently he brushed a fly from his face as he slumped forward, his eyes locked on the TV. Katie wondered if he even knew she was there.

Oh, well, I may as well expect a mountain to laugh, she thought, shaking her head ruefully at her stolid, heavy-set cousin.

"I can't believe it! Hot dog!" Aunt Rainie cried gleefully for about the zillionth time.

Katie just *had* to find out what was going on. Who was Aunt Rainie talking to? And what could they possibly be talking about to make Aunt Rainie shout like this?

Katie's aunt was a pretty constant phone chatterer, always talking to friends in her loud, amiable, animated way. Since coming to live here, Katie had grown used to Aunt Rainie's chortling guffaws and explosions of good-natured disbelief whenever she heard some piece of astounding local gossip.

But this sounded like something more. For one thing, Katie had never heard Aunt Rainie say "hot dog!" before. In fact, in her entire life, Katie had never really heard *anyone* say it.

Swinging her long legs off the couch, Katie walked into the kitchen just as her aunt hung up. Aunt Rainie whirled around and pressed her broad back against the wall. Her round, pleasant face radiated dazed bliss. Her skin nearly matched her bright fuschia muumuu. Her frizz of tight bleached blonde curls looked even wilder and more puffed out than usual, as if whatever news she had just heard had actually made her hair stand on end.

"Good lord," Aunt Rainie murmured, then "Hot dog!" she yelped one last time.

"What?" Katie asked. Aunt Rainie's happiness was so contagious Katie couldn't help grinning, even though she still didn't know what was going on.

Aunt Rainie smiled at Katie. From deep in her throat came a low chuckle that rumbled up and out until it became a full blown belly laugh.

"I won the sweepstakes!" she exploded. "Jeff and me are going to Hawaii! Hawaii, you hear?"

Aunt Rainie flew toward Katie and grabbed her hands. Hooting with glee, she danced Katie in a joyful circle. Katie tossed back her straight, auburn-brown ponytail and laughed along with her aunt as they twirled around the kitchen.

"Oops!" Aunt Rainie cried as she bumped a chair and it clattered down onto the floor.

Breathlessly, she stopped to right it. "Jeff and me ain't never been nowhere in our lives," she said, panting and leaning heavily on the chair. "I mean, we've been down to the city a few times and over to Miller's Creek, of course, but never anyplace exciting like Hawaii. When I saw that sweepstakes at the mall, something told me I just had to take a chance and—what do you know—I won it!"

Just then, a tall, strongly built man in his late fifties came through the door. His weathered, deeply lined face scowled in bewilderment at the sight of his happy, breathless wife and niece. "What's going on?" he asked, his voice low and gravelly as usual.

"Jeff, remember I told you I entered that contest at the mall?" Aunt Rainie said excitedly.

"No," Uncle Jeff replied bluntly, pulling off his heavy work gloves.

"Yes, you do, Jeff," Aunt Rainie insisted. "Remember you were all peeved off because I bought those sweepstakes tickets?"

"Oh, now I remember," said Uncle Jeff, his small blue-gray eyes widening. "You bought ten of those fool things! As if we have money to burn! I don't know what gets into you sometimes. We're sky-high with bills and you go off and waste ten dollars, buying a buncha fool—"

"I won," Aunt Rainie interrupted, softly.

Uncle Jeff's eyes narrowed. "What?"

"I won!" she shouted with enormous gusto. "We are going to Hawaii for two weeks and staying in a fancy hotel on the beach. And all it cost was the money I spent on those sweepstakes tickets! Ten little old dollars!" she finished triumphantly.

Katie chuckled as she watched Uncle Jeff's stern face twist into a series of changing expressions: disbelief, shock, amazement, a flicker of something unusual for him—a tiny ray of hopeful joy—then doubt. "Are you *sure* you won this thing?" he finally asked.

"I just got the call," Aunt Rainie told him. "It was Marilyn Snow, the manager of the Pine Ridge Mall her very self! Jeff, it's true!"

A broad smile cracked Uncle Jeff's face in an expression of all-out surprised happiness Katie had never seen her taciturn uncle wear. "Well, what do you know," he murmured wonderingly. "Hawaii."

Aunt Rainie wrapped her big, soft arms around him and squeezed tight. Then she took his arm and towed him into the living room. "Come on," she said, giggling, "let's go tell Mel our good news."

Seeing them so happy made Katie glad. *They deserve it*, she thought. She knew well enough they hadn't had an easy life. Like many people in their small farming community, they worked hard for their money—Aunt Rainie gave shampoos in a beauty salon and Uncle Jeff repaired farm machinery—and they didn't have a lot of it.

Katie gazed out the back door. Mel's big, black dog, Dizzy—a mixed breed of some kind, probably part Labrador retriever—lay dozing beside a low boulder near the side of the dirt path that led into the pine trees behind the house. Suddenly he lifted his head and sniffed the air alertly. Katie wondered what had caught his attention. Was it one of the fat raccoons that sometimes waddled out of the woods? Or was it just the cool, woodsy smell of autumn he now scented so intently?

Pushing the door open, Katie stepped outside. She shivered and pulled her hands up into the sleeves of her hooded gray sweatshirt to warm them. It had been a mild autumn so far, but she could feel it changing. The air was different somehow. Crisper. Chillier.

What a great time to be going to Hawaii, Katie thought as she wandered over toward Dizzy. Aunt Rainie and Uncle Jeff would be going away just in time to miss the colder weather that was surely coming.

Katie stopped short and covered her mouth as an unexpected memory stunned her. At first, she just heard the woman's voice—her mother's rich, soft voice. "I think the weather's changing, Tom. It's clouding up."

Then the picture filled Katie's mind. It was a picture of her life as it had been less than a year ago. She saw her mother parting the lace curtains in their apartment on West 68th Street and gazing out the window. How beautiful her face was, with her large brown eyes and her soft brown hair swinging to her chin.

Then Katie saw her father come up and put his hands on her mother's slim shoulders while he, too, looked out at the storm clouds gathering above the city skyline.

His warm eyes were amber brown, exactly like Katie's. She'd gotten her height and broad shoulders from him, too. "Don't worry. We'll have fun even if it rains," he assured Katie's mother.

Did they have fun? Katie wondered. She had no idea.

It had drizzled gloomily during their entire long weekend vacation at the beach. Katie remembered how she'd stayed at her friend Addy's house while they were away, how she and Addy had been stuck inside and bored stiff.

Then, on Monday night, as her parents were driving back, it had stormed wildly. Thunder. Lightning. A truck coming toward them on the narrow two-lane road swerved sharply to avoid driving into a jagged bolt of lightning that struck the wet road ahead of him. He didn't notice Katie's parents' car until . . .

After. Not until after it was too late. At least that's what he'd told the police.

Katie shook her head hard, as if to toss out the memory. She forced herself to start walking again. She didn't want to think about this anymore.

Everything's all right now, she told herself fiercely. *All that's over with.* Katie understood that her parents were never coming back from their vacation. She understood it in her heart now as well as in her head. It hadn't been easy. None of it had been.

But it was over.

Almost. The unbearable, deep pain had faded some, anyway. She was no longer afraid to cry. And when she *did* cry it no longer came in uncontrollable waves of bone-wracking misery.

Lately, she'd begun to feel like Aunt Rainie and Uncle Jeff, her mother's half sister and her husband, really were her family. They weren't as educated and as her own parents and they sure had a lot less money, but they weren't the weird country hillbillies she'd thought at first.

They'd taken her in, even though they barely knew her, because Aunt Rainie said, "Family is family." Katie knew Uncle Jeff hadn't been in favor of the idea. "Another mouth to feed." That's what she'd overheard him complaining to Aunt Rainie when she first arrived. But lately he seemed to be softening a little, almost as if he might like her. She could tell he was getting used to having her around, anyway. And Aunt Rainie was always warm to her. Then again, Aunt Rainie was warm to everyone. Katie didn't especially feel Aunt Rainie liked her any more than she liked the people whose hair she washed at the beauty salon. But she didn't like her any less. At least Aunt Rainie was a nice person. All in all, things weren't that bad.

Katie reached Dizzy and bent to pet him. As she did, the dog jumped to his feet, barking sharply at the trees. "Be quiet, you silly dog," Katie scolded fondly, but Dizzy kept barking.

Looking hard into the woods, Katie saw nothing. *Probably just a squirrel*, she thought as Dizzy darted off into the trees.

Though she couldn't see him, Katie could still hear him barking. From the sound, she could tell that he'd stopped running. He'd cornered something or had chased it up a tree.

"*What* is he barking at?" she wondered aloud as she walked toward the sharp, agitated yapping.

2

"*This* is what you're yipping about?" Dizzy danced excitedly in front of Katie, proud of his find.

Katie turned the plastic baby bottle in her hands. An inch or so of milk sloshed in its bottom. When she'd caught up with Dizzy among the trees, he'd had it cradled in his jaws.

Dizzy barked sharply at something off to the right. Katie looked, but saw no one. On three sides were trees, mostly the tall, brooding pines that seemed to grow everywhere in Pine Ridge. Behind her, through the trees, was the tumbledown, rust-red barn that her aunt and uncle used for storage. The nearest house was a nearly a quarter mile away.

Who had come through here? she wondered. Dizzy wouldn't have barked at an old bottle just lying on the ground. Someone had been out here, someone who had dropped a baby bottle.

"Katie!" a voice called from over by the barn. "Where are you?"

"Here," she shouted as she walked toward the barn with Dizzy trotting along beside her.

A petite girl in neat jeans and a crisp, lacy white shirt stood by the barn. Her mane of wild red curls tumbled around her slim shoulders. A wash of pale freckles accented her pretty, delicate features. She idly kicked at the dirt with one polished black boot as she looked around for Katie.

"Hi, Ashley," Katie called to her friend as she emerged from the trees.

Ashley's green eyes lit up in greeting at the sight of Katie. "Your aunt said you must be out here somewhere. What's that?"

"Dizzy, the great hunter, tracked down a baby bottle," Katie replied, handing it to Ashley.

Ashley unscrewed the cap and sniffed the bottle. "It smells okay," she mused. "It couldn't have been there for long. He found it in the woods, you said?"

Katie laughed. "Who are you? Nancy Drew?" she teased.

Ashley smiled as she shrugged good-naturedly. "I always wanted to be," she admitted.

Katie took the bottle from Ashley and hurled it back into the trees. "Whoever dropped it might come back looking for it," she said as the bottle flew in an arc and disappeared into the woods.

Dizzy jumped excitedly. Dead pine needles sprayed out from under his feet as he lunged back into the trees. "I don't believe it! He's going to go fetch it," Katie said, laughing and rolling her eyes. "Stay, Dizzy!" she called, but the dog paid no attention.

Katie turned toward Ashley. "What's up?"

"Nothing. My parents were going into town so I asked them to drop me off on the way. They'll pick me up on their way back. What's been going on around here anyway? When I stopped by the house you aunt was dancing all over the place like she just won the lottery or something."

"She practically did," Katie told her, grinning. "She won a two-week trip to Hawaii."

Ashley grabbed Katie's arm. "Oh, wow! That's incredible! You're going to Hawaii?"

"Naw, just Aunt Rainie and Uncle Jeff," Katie said, all her bad feelings flooding back.

"Oh," Ashley said, her own face falling. "Oh, well, that's too bad for you but nice for them, I guess. Hey!" she said, brightening, "maybe you could stay at my place while they're away."

An icy chill ran through Katie.

Maybe you could stay at my place.

She remembered her friend Addy saying the exact same thing. How excited she'd been to be sleeping over at Addy's place for the weekend. She'd been almost glad about her parents' vacation. She and Addy would have a blast.

That weekend the rain had dampened their plans to sneak up onto the roof of Addy's apartment building and sleep under the stars. But, still, even though it had sometimes been boring at Addy's, Katie had never for a moment worried that her parents might not return to her. It had never occurred to her at all.

Of course they would return. They always did.

Only that time, they didn't.

"Katie, what's the matter?" Ashley's concerned voice cut through Katie's dark memories. "All of a sudden you got so pale."

Katie blinked hard to bring herself back to the present. "Oh, sorry. I was just thinking about something. It's not important."

"Are you sure?" Ashley persisted. "You had a real funny look on your face there for a minute."

"Sure," Katie said casually. "Want to look in the barn?"

"Okay," Ashley agreed. "What's in it?"

"A lot of junk," Katie said honestly. "But, hey, the sign I told you about is in there! Want to see it?"

"The bridge sign?" Ashley's eyes widened. "The Angels Crossing bridge sign?"

"Yeah. Come on, I'll show you." Katie pushed on the barn's peeling red door. It creaked open complainingly.

"Wow! This place is really full of old stuff!" Ashley yelled as she followed Katie into the barn. Along the unpainted plank walls an assortment of items sat in haphazard piles: bits and pieces of old farm machinery, rusted car parts, and boxes upon boxes filled with old toys, dishes, and all sorts of other odds and ends. A broken dining room table lay on its side, its remaining legs jutting out. Old magazines were piled in dusty stacks.

The grime on the broken window overhead gave what light there was a soft grayness. The gray light always made Katie feel as if she'd stepped into an old photograph.

Katie led Ashley to a faded, frayed, rose-patterned chair in one corner of the barn. "This is my thinking chair," she told Ashley. "I come and sit out here when I want to be alone to think about stuff."

Ashley ran her hand along the worn material. "It's beautiful," she murmured. "I mean, if it was fixed up it would be," she added.

Katie nodded, pleased that Ashley could see the beauty in this broken-down old chair, just as she did. Katie knew her mother would have seen it, too. She'd have immediately seen its potential, dragged it out of the barn, and started repairing it. "Maybe I should fix it up," Katie considered aloud.

"That's a good idea," Ashley told her. "So where's the sign?"

Katie reached behind the chair and hauled up a plank of weathered wood. Two words were carved into it: Angels Crossing. "Ta-da," Katie sang out as she presented it to Ashley.

Ashley ran one perfectly manicured hand along the

letters as a dreamy look swept over her face. "It's funny, isn't it," she said after a moment. "If you hadn't discovered this sign in here one day, all the rest might not have happened."

"I never thought of it that way, but you're right," Katie mused. "If I hadn't found the sign, we'd never have gone looking for the bridge. And if we'd never gone looking for the bridge . . ." she trailed off.

"We'd never have met . . . *them*," Ashley finished.

Thoughtfully, Katie settled down into her chair. Uncle Jeff told her that his sister, Trudie, had come home from the Pine Manor woods carrying this sign one day. By the time Katie came upon it, it had been long forgotten in a messy pile of scrap wood.

The name had intrigued her. Angels Crossing.

It had reminded her of the zillions of Deer Crossing signs on the Pine Ridge roadsides. She'd giggled to herself, picturing a line of impatient drivers waiting with idling engines while tranquil, white-gowned angels with glistening wings floated gracefully across the road.

It had just seemed sort of amusing then. She couldn't possibly have known that the search for the bridge would lead her to real angels. Honest-to-goodness real angels.

But that's exactly what had happened. She knew she wasn't imagining it. Ashley and Christina, another friend, had seen them, too.

"You ought to hang this in your room," Ashley suggested.

"No," Katie said quickly, scowling as she shook her head.

"Why not?"

"I don't know," Katie said carefully. "Maybe I don't want to think about them every night before I go to bed."

"How come?"

"It's like . . . too much. I still have a hard time believing we really saw them," Katie added with an off-hand air.

"I kind of know what you mean, I guess. We did see them, though," Ashley said firmly.

"I know we did. Still, it's just not something I want to think about all the time." She paused and sat forward in her chair, looking into Ashley's trusting eyes. Ashley really listened when people spoke. Katie liked that about her. There was no reason to be guarded or secretive with her. She was a good friend, a true friend. "When I think about angels it makes me wonder about other . . . you know . . . other things that are . . . mysterious," she confided.

Ashley frowned in confusion. Katie knew she wasn't being clear.

"It makes me think of my parents," she blurted. "It makes me wonder if they're angels or ghosts or something. Or maybe they're just . . . gone."

At that moment, Dizzy scurried into the barn with the baby bottle in his jaws. Katie laughed as she took the bottle from him. "If I'd *wanted* him to fetch it, he'd never do it," she said.

Ashley and Katie spent the next hour browsing through the dusty, faded magazines. Some were very old, from the time when Aunt Rainie was a teenager. Others were newer. They'd probably belonged to Aunt Rainie and Uncle Jeff's grown daughters who lived with their husbands over in Miller's Creek.

The two friends were laughing at the outrageous neon styles in a fashion magazine from 1974, when Aunt Rainie came into the barn with two icy-cold cans of soda. "Thought you might like these," she said, handing them each one.

She glanced over their shoulders at the magazine. "Those were some times," she commented. Katie wasn't sure if she liked the clothing on the page or not. In Katie's opinion, Aunt Rainie had really, well, *loud* taste in clothing.

"Time goes so fast," Aunt Rainie said with a wistful sigh. Then her face brightened. "Katie, I called and made all the travel arrangements. Uncle Jeff and I will be leaving for Hawaii next week."

"Next week?" Katie cried in surprise. "Why are you going so soon?"

"Jeff says things are slow at work right now, so it's probably the best time for him to be away. It doesn't matter to me. I can always get someone to cover my hours at the beauty parlor."

"But next week just seems, uh, so soon," Katie protested, her heart racing.

They couldn't go next week! It was too . . . too sudden!

She hadn't expected them to just get up and go like, like *this*. As long as their trip had seemed far in the future it hadn't seemed so scary. But now it *was* scary. Too scary.

"Katie can stay at my place," Ashley eagerly suggested to Aunt Rainie.

"Oh, thanks, but we wouldn't want to put your folks out like that. Katie can stay here with Mel," Aunt Rainie said. She turned toward Katie. "We trust you, Katie, and we know you'll mind Mel."

Katie couldn't picture herself taking orders from Mel. But, then again, she couldn't picture Mel *giving* orders, either. He'd probably just sit and watch TV the whole week. The only time he'd even notice his parents were gone was at meal time.

"I guess it will be all right," Katie agreed cautiously.

"Hellooooo?" a woman's voice called from outside the barn.

"That's Mom," Ashley said, jumping to her feet. "I'll see you in school on Monday, Katie. Bye, Mrs. Stoppelmeyer," she told Aunt Rainie. "Congratulations on winning that trip to Hawaii."

"Thanks," Aunt Rainie said, waving as Ashley hurried to the pretty blonde woman waiting in the open doorway.

Aunt Rainie glanced at the baby bottle, still sitting where Katie had put it on the dirty cement floor. "Where did that come from?" she asked, blinking in surprise.

"Dizzy found it in the woods," Katie told her.

Picking it up, Aunt Rainie gazed fondly at the bottle. "Babies are so darling," she breathed.

"I guess so, yeah," Katie answered, disinterested. She couldn't think about babies now. She was too busy fighting down the panic sweeping through her. She wasn't being reasonable, she told herself. Something so awful as losing a second set of parents just wouldn't happen. The odds had to be incredible that it could ever happen again.

Impulsively, Katie put a hand on her aunt's wide arm.

"What, Katie?" Aunt Rainie asked, concerned. "What is it?" she asked tenderly. "Are you okay? Tell me, please, sweetheart. What's wrong?"

I don't want you to go. Those were the words that sprang to Katie's mind. It didn't seem right to say them, though. It would be babyish and selfish.

"I'll miss you," she simply said instead.

"Ahhh!" Aunt Rainie put her arm around Katie and squeezed. "That's so sweet of you to say, honey. We'll miss you, too, you know."

Katie basked in the warm security of being enfolded in her aunt's affectionate hug. *She'll come back*, Katie told herself as she held her aunt tightly. *They'll come back. They've got to.*

Later that night, thought, as Katie sat in bed and cuddled her gray tabby kitten, Nagle, her uneasiness began to creep back. She felt edgy and unsettled.

Nagle clawed playfully at the sleeve of her blue flannel nightshirt. Katie rolled him onto his back and ruffled the soft white fur on his belly. Nagle was so sweet and special to her. She loved the way he purred as he curled up next to her at night. She loved the way his softly pattering feet greeted her each day whenever she returned to the house.

Was she special to him? Katie wondered.

Was she special to anyone?

She *had* been when her parents were still alive. She'd been a special, treasured only daughter. But now she was a responsibility. Aunt Rainie and Uncle Jeff's responsibility. It was probably to their credit that they took her in, that they lived up to their responsibility. But still, it wasn't the same as being special.

Katie reached under her bed and took out the black-and-white covered notebook she used as a journal. Taking out the pen she'd left in the middle of the notebook, she began to write.

Dear Journal,

Alone again. Aunt Rainie and Uncle Jeff will be going away on vacation. I bet they'll be glad not to have a kid around for awhile. All their kids are grown. If I hadn't come along, they wouldn't have to worry about kids anymore. I wonder how they feel about me. I mean, really feel. I'm not sure. Do they love me? I don't think so. They treat me all right, but I don't think anyone can love you the way your own parents do. It would be nice to be loved like that again. I remember feeling like my parents loved me like crazy. I don't feel that way now. I guess I never will feel that way again.

3

The week passed quickly. Too quickly. Katie felt that, in a blink, Aunt Rainie and Uncle Jeff were packed and leaving for Hawaii.

"I am not wearing this fool thing!" Uncle Jeff bellowed.

Katie had been on her way downstairs, but now she couldn't help stopping in the hallway outside her aunt and uncle's bedroom to listen. Their door was half open so it was easy to hear. In fact, Uncle Jeff was yelling so loud, it would have been no problem even if the door had been shut.

"Oh, Jeff, don't be such an old poop!" Aunt Rainie scolded in a laughing voice. "I bought it 'specially for the trip. It looks great. Don't be such a crabby old man."

Hmmmm, Katie wondered. Uncle Jeff could be pretty crabby. But then, Aunt Rainie did have extremely questionable taste. What could Uncle Jeff be wearing?

Cautiously, she peeked into their room. Her hand flew over her mouth as she stifled her laughter. Uncle Jeff stood ramrod straight, looking completely miserable in an oversize Hawaiian shirt. Flying fish in neon colors covered the material in a dizzying pattern. *That shirt's so bad it's cool*, Katie thought as a giggle escaped her lips.

"It makes you look ten years younger," said Aunt Rainie, straightening the collar. She herself was dressed in a flowing, gauzy, blindingly neon green sundress. Katie was used to seeing Aunt Rainie in bright colors. They were all she ever wore. But Uncle Jeff *never* wore them. Overalls and workshirts pretty much made up his whole wardrobe. "You look very handsome," Aunt Rainie said confidently.

Uncle Jeff turned and caught sight of Katie peering in the doorway. His weathered brow furrowed into a deep frown. "What are you smiling at, girlie-girl?" he barked.

Katie didn't trust herself to answer. She hiccuped with suppressed laughter and scurried past the door and down the stairs.

Downstairs, Mel lounged in a kitchen chair with his legs up on a second and third chair, talking on the wall phone. "Listen, Mary Ellen, I'll be there as soon as I can. I gotta look at the brakes on my bike first. I'm just really busy right now."

Katie shook her head in disbelief. Busy? Mel? That would be the day. Mel never rushed for anything. He was the king of hanging out, doing nothing. But if his precious motorcycle needed work then he *would* consider that a crisis. It would require him to muster some brainpower, which would probably strike him as being very taxing. He might *think* he was busy.

"I'll be over when I get the chance, Mary Ellen," Mel repeated impatiently.

In Katie's opinion, Mel's girlfriend, Mary Ellen, was all right. Katie had no idea what she could possibly see in Mel.

"Spud's coming over with his pickup to take the bike down to his shop," Mel told Mary Ellen. "I don't know how long it will take. I just don't know, M.E., so quit asking, okay?"

Uncle Jeff and Aunt Rainie came into the kitchen. Stubborn Uncle Jeff had changed into a starchy, long-sleeved white shirt and faded, but sharply creased black pants. He carried a bulging leather suitcase. "Well, this is it," he said awkwardly. "We're leaving."

Aunt Rainie bent to fix something on the hem of her dress. When she looked up, her eyes met Katie's. "I have something for you," she said.

Guiding Katie into the living room, Aunt Rainie sat on the worn couch. "I found this in an old album and I had it reproduced at the Photo Deluxe in the mall." She handed a photograph to Katie.

Katie looked down at the smiling couple in the photo. Her parents. They looked young. The picture was probably taken before she was even born. Katie could see a lake and mountains in the background.

"They were on their honeymoon here," Aunt Rainie explained. "Your mom sent me the picture in a note she sent thanking me for their wedding gift. I thought you might like to have it."

Of course she would like to have it. She'd *love* to have it. "Thanks," said Katie. "I only have one picture of them."

"You do?" cried Aunt Rainie. "That's terrible. There must be me than that. I think maybe your Aunt Lorna might have the photo albums. Or maybe Uncle Frank has them. I'll try to find out for you."

Katie nodded. "Okay. Thanks." She felt strange. Aunt Rainie's unexpected gesture—and the surprising sensitivity behind it—really touched Katie. But she was half-afraid to show it. Especially now, it was important to Katie to be able to at least pretend Aunt Rainie and Uncle Jeff didn't matter all that much to her. Otherwise, she just couldn't trust herself not to break down and sob at their leaving.

Aunt Rainie wasn't finished, though. "I thought you might like to have this, too," she said softly after a minute or two. She dug in her purse and pulled out a beautiful, curlicued chain with a round silver circle attached. "It's a locket," she said, using her long hot-pink nails to gently pry it open. "It's real silver, Katie, and real old, too. My mom, your grandmother, gave it to me. I never used it and I thought you might like it."

Katie took the locket from Aunt Rainie. Sometimes she almost forgot that Aunt Rainie and her mother had the same mother. Katie had never known her grandmother because she had died before Katie was born. Her mother and Aunt Rainie had different fathers, and they didn't even know each other all that well. They seemed like complete opposites, but if Katie looked carefully at Aunt Rainie she could definitely see her resemblance to Katie's mother.

"You could put your parents' pictures in there if you want," Aunt Rainie suggested gently. "It'd be a real family keepsake for you, sweetheart."

For a moment, Katie blinked back tears as she studied the two small frames of the open locket, then, with a whooshing breath, she snapped it shut. "Thanks, Aunt Rainie," she said, impulsively wrapping her arms around her aunt's neck. "Thanks a lot."

"Rainie, get a move on!" Uncle Jeff shouted from the kitchen. Katie followed Aunt Rainie into the kitchen, and Uncle Jeff eyed her sternly. "Now I don't want to hear about you skipping school, or staying out late, or any other high jinks while we're away."

"Jeff, you know we trust Katie," Aunt Rainie said.

"Just the same," Uncle Jeff insisted.

"No problem. I'm cool," Katie assured them. "But, remember, I have off on Monday. Teachers' conference."

"Oh, that's right," Aunt Rainie recalled.

Uncle Jeff jabbed Mel in the arm. "You, neither. No crazy parties, no nothin'. We're leaving you in charge, hear?" he said, scowling.

"No sweat," Mel mumbled.

"Well, Rainie, let's go. We don't want to miss our plane," Uncle Jeff said, picking up their suitcase. "You two be good."

Aunt Rainie hugged Katie, then Mel. "See you soon! We'll be sure to send a postcard," she trilled in a happy singsong voice as she followed Uncle Jeff out the door.

Katie waved, looking down at the scuffed green-and-white linoleum. She couldn't bear to watch them go. It felt too weird, as if yet another chapter of her life were abruptly ending.

Wandering back into the living room, Katie plunked down on the couch. She opened and closed her locket several times. She leaned forward and opened a drawer in the wood coffee table in front of the couch. Plucking out a small pair of scissors, she began carefully cutting the photo of her parents. When she had a circle with her mother's face and one with her father's, she slipped the photos into the locket frames. As she got to her feet, she draped the chain over her head and snapped the locket shut.

"Now what do I do?" she asked herself aloud. Maybe she'd go see what Ashley and Christina were doing. Yeah, that would be a good idea. "Oh, Melvin, honey, darling, dear," she sang out as she strolled into the kitchen.

She found Mel casually digging through the refrigerator. Turning, he came up biting into a cold chicken drumstick. "Don't call me Melvin," he mumbled, his mouth full of chicken. "And I can't take you nowheres because the bike is busted." Sometimes Mel would drive Katie places, especially if she paid him.

"Spud's coming with his pickup, isn't he?" she reminded him. "And the ranch is on the way to his garage." Ashley's parents owned the Pine Manor Horse Ranch. Christina and her mother lived on the ranch, too, since Alice Kramer, Christina's mother, worked there.

Mel belched and tossed a hunk of chicken across the kitchen to Dizzy, who rested by the doorway. "I guess you could have a ride," he muttered grudgingly.

A half hour later, a dented brown pickup truck rattled to a stop on the dirt drive outside the house. Mel went out to greet Spud, a stocky young man with a shaggy beard. Together, they lifted Mel's motorcycle onto the truck.

"Want to ride in the back?" Spud asked Katie.

Katie smiled. She liked Spud even though she thought his tattoos and the red bandanna he tied around his head made him look like a lunatic who thought he was a pirate.

She'd always thought it would be cool to ride in the open back of a pickup. Still, she knew she shouldn't. "It's not really safe, is it?" Katie asked, even though she already knew it wasn't.

"No, but you're not going far," Spud said. "It's better than being squished in the front seat."

Katie eagerly agreed to sit in the back with the motorcycle. After all, his might be her only chance. She knew full well her aunt and uncle would never permit it. But now they weren't there to stop her, and Mel certainly didn't care.

Swinging her long legs over the tailgate, Katie climbed into the pickup. Spud started the engine and the truck began moving down the bumpy dirt drive that led to the busier main road.

Katie turned the collar of her denim jacket up to protect her from the chilly wind whipping her hair around her face. She felt independent and free. So what if Aunt Rainie and Uncle Jeff didn't come back? She didn't need them. She could take care of herself.

Sitting in the back with the motorcycle made her feel totally cool.

She hoped someone she knew would see her.

4

Someone did see her.

"Thanks for the ride and, uh, sorry, Spud," Katie said as she climbed out of the cab of the pickup, which had stopped in front of Ashley's neat ranch-style house.

"It wasn't your fault," Spud replied, unconcerned. A motorcycle-riding police officer had pulled Spud over almost the second they were out on the main road. He'd insisted that Katie get out of the back and then issued Spud a ticket. "That cop just seemed to come out of nowhere," Spud added, shaking his head in disbelief. "Like he just *appeared* or something."

"Traffic cops are like that," Mel remarked sagely.

Katie stood on the metal running board outside the cab and talked to Spud through the window and across Mel. "I'll help you pay the ticket. It's really my fault."

"No ticket," Spud reported with a grin.

"I saw him give you one," said Katie, her eyes wide with surprise. Katie was sure. After all, she'd been there. She'd seen it happen, even read the policeman's nameplate: Officer Winger.

Spud shook his head. "As I was pulling away I looked in my rearview mirror and I saw him ripping up the ticket."

"You were seeing things," Mel scoffed.

"I don't think so," Spud said.

"Why would a cop give you a ticket and then rip it up?" Mel demanded.

"Maybe he just wanted me to be safe," Katie suggested as she hunched further into her jacket to keep out the cool breeze.

"Yeah, *right*," Mel guffawed. "That's *real* believable. You'd better pay that ticket, Spud, or you'll be in trouble."

"If you do pay it, I'll split it with you," Katie offered, jumping down onto the dirt road. "Bye. Thanks again for the ride."

The pickup turned and headed back down the road. As she watched it disappear, Katie wondered about Officer Winger. He'd been awfully polite and pleasant. She could believe he'd rip up the ticket—although she didn't think police officers usually did that sort of thing. Yet, he'd been *so* nice, even smiled and offered his hand as she'd climbed out of the back of the truck.

A sharp tap on her shoulder startled Katie and she whirled around.

"Sorry," said Ashley. "I didn't mean to scare you. I didn't know you were coming over."

"I figured there was no sense in calling you. No one's ever inside your house on a Saturday afternoon, anyway." Weekends were always busy at the ranch. Ashley's entire family—mother, father, Ashley, and her twin brothers—worked outside, tending the horses, maintaining the grounds, or taking customers out on trail rides through the Pine Manor woods just behind the stable.

Over the summer Katie had worked in the bunkhouse across the way where guests stayed over. But, now that it was fall and there were fewer guests, Mr. and Mrs. Kingsley had laid off all but a few staff members.

"I have to help Alice take out a trail ride," Ashley said. She nodded toward the stable just across the way. A group of people milled about while, one by one, Alice led out saddled horses and helped the riders to mount. "I'd really better go. Want to come for a ride?"

"Not really," Katie replied. She was new to riding and wasn't totally at ease on horseback. Today she wasn't in the mood to be uneasy. Aunt Rainie and Uncle Jeff's departure had already unnerved her enough.

"Where's Christina?" Katie asked. Since Ashley was busy, maybe Christina would be able to hang out with Katie.

"She's at her house doing an astrological chart for Molly Morgan."

"Molly Morgan!" Katie cried incredulously.

Ashley delicately wrinkled her freckled nose in

distaste. "I know. It's weird. Ever since Molly came out of the hospital, they've been hanging out together sometimes. I don't understand it," she sighed.

From Ashley's expression Katie could tell she didn't like it, either. Ashley and Christina were practically like sisters. They'd lived together on the ranch since they were small. Katie could understand why Ashley wouldn't like the idea of someone else getting between Christina and herself.

It had been different with Katie. She'd started out as Ashley's friend. Then, more slowly, she'd gotten friendly with Christina through Ashley. So the Molly Morgan thing bothered Katie, but not as much as it would Ashley.

There was another problem, too. It was Molly Morgan herself. Ashley couldn't stand her. Actually, none of them could stand her in the beginning. She was vain, rude, and snobbish.

But lately all that had changed. Ever since Christina and Molly had met an angel in the woods, Molly was like a different person. She'd also gone into the hospital right afterwards to be treated for anorexia, an eating disorder.

It was two weeks since Molly had come out of the hospital, and the change in her was startling. The extra pounds she'd gained had even improved her already good looks. Molly's wiry, sharp-featured beauty was softened. She looked prettier, seemed more approachable. Her pointy face had been gentled.

That was how Katie saw it. Ashley didn't agree.

"I still don't trust her," Ashley said. "Christina's kind-

hearted and Molly thinks she can push her around."
Shielding her eyes against the sun, Ashley glanced over
at the stable. People were gathering, waiting to go out
on their ride. "I'd better go," she said. "See you later."

"Later," Katie said, waving as Ashley walked off. She
headed down the dirt road past Ashley's house to a
small cabin set back a little bit off the road.

At Katie's knock, a pretty girl with wavy corn-colored
hair answered the door. Her sky-blue eyes brightened as
she greeted Katie. "Hi. Come on in," she said, pulling
open the door.

Katie entered the cozy, rustic cabin. Molly sat on the
cushiony brown couch facing the fireplace. Katie
nodded a hello.

"Hi, Katie," Molly greeted her pleasantly. Her white-
blonde hair was pulled back in its usual French braid.
Even though her shirt and jeans hung casually on her
slim frame, there was something about the way Molly
wore clothing that made her look as if she'd walked
right out of a fashion magazine.

"It's because even her socks cost a hundred dollars,"
Ashley had once remarked scornfully. Katie sensed
some jealousy there since Ashley loved clothes herself,
but couldn't afford the kind of expensive clothing Molly
could.

"Molly is a double Virgo with Scorpio rising,"
Christina reported.

Katie rolled her eyes. "What the heck is that supposed
to mean?" she blurted. Katie thought astrology was a

complete waste of time and energy. As far as she was concerned, it made no sense at all.

Christina adored it, though. In Katie's opinion, Christina was interested in all kinds of weird stuff. In fact, it always seemed to Katie that the weirder it was, the more Christina went for it.

Christina leaned on the counter that separated the kitchen from the living room. She raised her blonde eyebrows, wrinkling the small white scar in her left eyebrow, the only mark that remained from a spill off a horse. "I know you don't believe any of this. But, since you asked, it means . . ." She picked up a piece of paper she'd been writing on and read from it. "Molly is intelligent, creative, and adaptable. The influence of Scorpio makes her very strong-willed and somewhat vain."

"That sounds right," Molly agreed.

"Oh, you could say that about anybody," Katie scoffed.

"No," Christina disagreed. "You're not vain at all. I couldn't say it about you."

"Well, almost anybody," Katie insisted, self-consciously smoothing her windblown auburn hair. She sat beside Molly on the couch, stretching her long legs out on under the coffee table. "Are you guys almost done with this?" she asked.

"Not really," Christina said with a sigh. "I've only calculated the placement of her inner planets so far. I have to chart the—"

"Never mind," Katie said, getting to her feet. This all seemed so silly to her that she didn't want to hear any more. It was true, Christina had great intuitions about things. She had *feelings* which were often true. But, that was as much as Katie could accept. The rest of it just usually annoyed her.

Then again, there were the angels. Christina had believed in them even when Katie hadn't. Then angels were true. There was no doubt of that in Katie's head anymore. She'd seen them. More than once.

Still, enough was enough. And all this astrology junk was too much.

Katie pulled open the front door. "I'll see you."

"Where are you going?" Christina asked.

"Out . . . I don't know. Out for a walk, I guess. I have some things I want to think about," Katie replied.

"Do you need to talk?" Christina asked, concerned.

"Naw," Katie said with a dismissive wave of her hand. Then she paused. Christina was a good person to talk to sometimes, partly because of her unusual outlook on things. "Well, I don't know. Maybe . . . Later, maybe."

"We'll be here," Christina said. "What's the matter?"

"Oh, Aunt Rainie and Uncle Jeff left today on their vacation and I'm just feeling . . . weird. You know, weird about it. But I'm okay. Yeah. I'm okay," Katie said quickly.

"If you're sure," Christina said.

"Yeah. Finish your chart and I'll come back later," Katie assured her.

"Okay," Christina said doubtfully. "If you're really sure."

Katie stepped out onto the dirt road and pulled the elastic from her ponytail, letting her hair swing free. Jamming her hands in her jacket pockets, she headed toward the stable.

A walk would do her good. It would give her time to think, to throw off this shaky feeling of being all alone in the world.

Besides, even if Aunt Rainie and Uncle Jeff never returned . . . even if they didn't, she'd manage. It wasn't like they were giving her such a great life right now, Katie tried to convince herself. The house could use some serious work. Uncle Jeff was a cheapskate and a grouch most of the time. Aunt Rainie was nice, of course, but she was sort of dizzy.

It wouldn't be any big loss.

At the stable, Katie peeked in through the top half of the double door. She inhaled the musty, oddly appealing smell of hay and horses. Right now most of the horses were out on trail rides.

Pushing off from the door, Katie went around to the back of the stable. For a moment, she stopped and stared at the thick pine trees rustling in the cool breeze. The wind carried the pine scent to her like an enticement to enter.

Katie sighed. Did she really want to go into the woods? So many strange things had happened there.

Sure. Why not? she thought with a defiant toss of her head. The woods was the perfect place for a walk. The perfect place to forget about everything.

5

Brown, brittle pine needles, the accumulation of countless passing years, crunched under the soles of her scuffed, tan work boots as Katie crested the hill. The lively music of rushing water in the rocky creek below played through the pines.

The cool shade of the woods gave way to a wide path of brilliant light where the trees parted to let the creek wind its way through. Spanning the gurgling, splashing creek with its foamy sun-flecked spray was an old, weather-beaten, covered bridge.

The Angels Crossing Bridge.

Whatever road had once led to and from this bridge had long since been overgrown with trees. The bridge was the only evidence of its having ever existed.

Why am I here? Katie wondered as she looked down at the pitched roof and open sides of the wooden bridge. Was she looking for angels? Did she need them?

Katie shook her head in silent answer to her own unspoken question. No. What did *she* need angels for? Nothing, that's what. Everything was under control.

Still, almost as if her feet had a mind of their own, she found herself walking toward the bridge.

Caw! The sharp sound made her turn to find its source. With a dramatic display of wide, shiny black wings, three crows skimmed the creek about three feet above the water. Abruptly, they rose in unison and settled on the very top of the bridge.

Shouting its shrill call one more time, one of the crows flapped its glistening wings as if showing off.

Katie stopped to look at them for a moment, then continued down to the bridge. The old boards creaked as soon as she stepped onto them. She stopped and leaned heavily on one of the bridge's thick, rough wooden supports. The light on the moving water below sparkled and leapt before her eyes.

She loved this bridge, she realized. It was a place she shared with Ashley and Christina, her two best friends. Now Molly knew about it, too. That was all right, really. Molly wasn't so bad, just lonely.

Katie scanned the bridge and recalled the first time she'd met Ned, Norma, and Edwina here. They hadn't seemed like angels at all, just odd, quirky characters playing cards—of all things—on a bridge in the middle of nowhere. But they *were* angels. Later, she'd seen them in all their shining majesty. It was a vision of beauty and light she'd never forget.

Leaning over the railing, Katie breathed deeply, drinking in the sweet, pine-scented air. As she leaned, the silver locket around her neck swung forward, dangling over the creek. Katie clasped it with one hand. If it were to suddenly come undone and slip into the water below, Katie would never forgive herself.

When she was back under the rooftop, she pulled the locket over her head. With a snap, she opened it and gazed fondly down at the photos of her mother and father. The sunlight glanced off the silvery frame around their smiling faces.

Even now, so many months later, she still half expected them to come back for her. She imagined that someday she'd wake up in Uncle Jeff and Aunt Rainie's house and hear her parents' voices downstairs in the kitchen. "Thanks for taking Katie for us while we were gone," she could imagine her father saying.

"I can't wait to see her," she could almost hear her mother say.

Suddenly, Katie sensed a presence, someone staring at her. Looking up sharply, she drew in a short, startled breath.

A crow eyed her intently as it stood silently on the railing beside her. It studied her, its head turning with quick, curious, jerky movements.

It's the locket, she realized, remembering that crows liked shiny objects.

Caw! the crow screamed as it unexpectedly leapt along the railing, moving closer to her.

Katie jumped back, a little frightened. "Go away!" she shouted, shooing it with her arms. "Get lost!"

The crow wasn't intimidated. It stood a moment more, then screeched its harsh call once again as it spread its wings and flew at her in a flurry of black feathers.

Katie cried out in alarm. Instinctively, she threw her arms up to shield herself from the crow.

Noiselessly, the locket slithered through her fingers.

With a wild flapping of wings, the crow dove for the locket.

"No!" Katie cried, lunging at the feathered thief. Her fingertips grazed one wing as it flew past her to perch on a crossbeam, the silvery locket dangling from its beak.

Katie leapt into the air, uselessly waving her arms in frustration. "Drop that!" she ordered the bird. "Drop it!"

The bird flew from the beam, out through the opening in the side of the bridge. It settled several yards down the creek on a fallen pine tree, now mostly covered in the rushing waters of the creek.

Dashing out the far end of the bridge, Katie rushed down to the water's edge and made her way quickly along the rocky bank. Behind her, the other two gleaming black crows sat watching from the bridge rooftop. Ahead, the thieving crow perched on a pine bough, the locket still in its beak.

Katie glanced at the rushing creek. If the locket dropped into the rushing water, it would be almost impossible to retrieve. The water was fiercely cold this time of year. And what if the swift current carried it away? She'd never find it again.

With a taunting squawk, the crow rose off the branch and flew farther down the creek. Katie hurried after it, her feet sliding on the wet stones.

After five more minutes of running, Katie lost sight of the bird. Looking around breathlessly, she found herself standing at a place where the water cascaded down a rock wall for about seven feet before settling into a swirling pool. Looking across the frothy pool, Katie saw another waterfall on the opposite side, probably from a different creek. There, too, the water became a shimmering silver curtain as it tumbled down the glistening, wet rocks.

"Wow," Katie murmured, mesmerized by the beauty of the spot and momentarily forgetting her locket.

The sound of chirping made her look up and she saw a small red and brown finch winging its way from one pine to another. As she focused on the bird, she saw that many different birds had congregated around the pool: black and gray chickadees, small gray tufted titmice, and sparrows.

For a moment, she thought she'd caught sight of the crow perched on a pine branch, but then noticed the brilliant patch of red at the top of one wing. It was a smaller bird, a red-winged blackbird.

A spark of vivid yellow flashed through the trees. It was a goldfinch, not yet reverted to its dull winter brown.

As her own breathing quieted, Katie was able to hear the varied songs of the birds above the rush of the water. She felt herself being lulled into a dreamy, happy state by her surroundings. It was hard to explain, just a feeling—as if all her worries weren't really that serious.

The feeling suddenly evaporated when a sharp caw overhead snapped her to attention. The crow sat on the very end of a rock ledge that jutted out through the cascading water on the far side of the pool. The silver locket dangled tauntingly from its beak. The spray from the waterfall made both the crow and the locket shine.

Katie gasped as the crow opened its beak. In what seemed like slow motion, the locket slipped from its beak and disappeared into the shimmering curtain of the waterfall.

Now it's gone forever! she thought miserably. "No," she said aloud, shaking off her despair. "I can still get it."

Setting her mouth in a determined line, Katie bent, unlaced her boots, and hurriedly kicked them off. She pushed her jeans up her legs and waded into the swirling pool. "Whoa, boy," she puffed with a violent shiver. The water was like ice and swirled around her legs with unexpected force.

In minutes, her legs were numb with cold and her teeth began to chatter. She found it hard to keep her balance. But Katie wasn't going to let some dumb crow beat her.

She reached the far waterfall, pulled off her denim jacket, and tied it around her waist. She pushed up the long sleeves of her blue T-shirt and prepared to reach into the frothy bottom of the waterfall. Maybe she'd be lucky and feel the locket before the cold became too unbearable.

Just as she reached out toward the waterfall, Katie stopped short, all her senses alert. A very strange sound had suddenly pierced the air around her. She wasn't sure what it was, but it was very, very close by.

6

It's a bobcat! Katie decided, alarmed by the unearthly shrieking. Uncle Jeff had warned her to be on the lookout for them when she was in the woods.

His words came back to her. "Used to be lots of nasty old bobs around, still some left. Ted Banner saw one by his chicken coop last week."

Why was it shrieking like that? Was it a mating call? Was it in pain?

A spray of freezing water jolted Katie. If it was a bobcat she should get out of here. A cat wouldn't go after her in the water, but she couldn't stay in too long or she'd freeze to death.

The frightening howl rang relentlessly through the woods.

"Wait!" Katie gasped as new realization hit her. *It's a baby. It might be.*

No, it had to be a bobcat. What would a baby be doing this far out in the woods?

The shrieking became louder. At least it seemed to.

Katie suddenly remembered the baby bottle Dizzy had found in the woods near the house. But if it was a baby, surely it had parents. If it was a baby, why didn't the parents do something?

Cocking her head attentively, Katie listened hard. The cries were so compelling, she couldn't ignore them.

But my locket. She glanced at the waterfall and back over her shoulder at the spinning pool. *I'll just check out these cries and come right back*, she decided. Her locket probably wouldn't go too far in a short amount of time.

She pulled herself onto the bank of the pool. Her soaked jeans felt clumsy and heavy as she quickly pulled on her socks and boots.

The screaming continued.

Where was it coming from? It had to be close by.

Dripping wet and shivering, Katie climbed up the rocky side of the waterfall.

At the top, the change in the woods was startling. White birches stood side by side, their white bark shining, their pale yellow autumn leaves shimmering in the breeze. Katie had never before seen anything but pines in this woods.

She walked through the birch trees, looking around herself on all sides. The awful shrieking grew louder. Katie was approaching the source.

Katie neared a mossy boulder between two birches and froze. Whatever was making the noise was behind the boulder.

Cautiously, Katie flattened herself against the cool rock and moved closer to the sound. Peering over the boulder, she cried out in surprise.

A red-faced baby in a pink one-piece stretchy suit sat propped against the boulder, screaming wildly.

Katie quickly checked around. Where were the parents? There was no sign of anyone but the baby.

"Poor baby," Katie cooed as she rushed to pick up the screeching child. The moment she lifted it up, its yowling subsided to pitiful breathy sobs.

Katie rocked gently and patted the baby's heaving back. "It's all right," she crooned. "It's all right."

Fat tears rolled down the baby's chubby cheeks. Her wet eyes gleamed, reminding Katie of a stone she'd seen in the nature store at the Pine Ridge Mall: hematite, a shiny black rock with flecks of shifting colors that changed as you rolled it in your hand.

She ran her hand across the dark, fuzzy wisps of hair on the baby's warm head. "Don't cry. Your mom will be right back."

Wouldn't she?

7

The light was dying. Shadows of deep magenta, wavering dark purple, and rich forest green slowly advanced, blanketing the once sun-dappled scenery.

Katie had waited in the woods with the baby for a long time. She wasn't sure how long because she didn't wear a watch.But she could tell from the light that it was getting late.

A brisk gust of wind ruffled the trees and sent a shower of pale yellow birch leaves fluttering to the ground. Katie shivered. Her jeans were still wet from wading into the pool, and her hair and shirt were damp from the waterfall spray.

The baby in her arms hooted in a high, loud voice, calling to Katie for attention. Katie looked down and tickled her under her chubby, soft chin. The baby chortled, revealing two small white teeth at the center of her bottom gums.

Again, the baby cried out, not unhappily, but as if she were trying to say something, to ask a question. "You don't know me, do you?" Katie spoke softly to the baby, instinctively using a more musical voice than her own natural one. "It's okay. I'm a friend. Don't worry."

The baby frowned, her smooth brow wrinkling, her expression still questioning. Katie felt like she should do something to communicate, but what?

A lullaby might reassure her. Babies liked lullabies. "Hi, hi, my angel pie," Katie crooned a lullaby her mother used to sing to her. It was the only one she still remembered because even after she was no longer a baby, her mother had often greeted her that way.

"Hi, hi, my angel pie."

Katie paused, trying to recall the next verse. The baby looked up at her expectantly with her trusting, hematite eyes.

The next verse was something about barefoot angels at the gates of heaven. Someone was making little shoes for them, Katie seemed to remember. She wasn't quite sure.

The baby gurgled at Katie in soft, unintelligible baby talk.

Katie leaned closer to listen. "What are you saying, little baby-baby? Where's your mama, huh?"

Peering around, Katie looked again for any clue she might have missed when she first searched the area— something that would tell her where this baby's parents had gone or who they were.

Her earlier search had revealed only the ashes of a burned out campfire and a brown grocery bag containing a small plastic flashlight, another stretchy suit, a pacifier, and a small, faded, rag doll.

Suddenly, Katie spotted something she'd overlooked before. A white cylinder lay among the mat of fallen birch leaves on the ground.

Stooping with the baby nestled in the crook of her arm, Katie picked it from the leaves. A baby bottle, exactly like the one Dizzy had brought her. There was still some liquid in it, about half a bottle full.

Katie unscrewed the cap and smelled the liquid. It smelled okay. Wrinkling her nose and preparing for the worst, she cautiously sipped it. Not bad. It wasn't milk, though. Baby formula or something, probably.

The baby began to fuss, moving her head from side to side while making small cranky grumbles. "Okay, okay," Katie said gently as she carefully put the top back on and brushed the nipple clean on her shirt. "Here you go." Katie lifted the nipple to the baby's lips. Instantly the infant took hold, voraciously guzzling the liquid.

Katie laughed softly, pleased that she'd found a way to make the baby happy. She moved to the boulder and slid to the ground with her back against the mossy rock. As the baby drank, Katie felt her small, impossibly soft hand wrap around Katie's thumb, her grip surprisingly strong.

"Aahh," Katie sighed happily. The baby was *so* sweet. A new feeling swept through Katie. She wasn't sure what it was. She felt this way when she cuddled her kitten, Nagle. But the feeling she had now was much stronger, as if something in her heart had actually, physically moved.

When the bottle was nearly empty, the baby's eyes grew heavy and her black-lashed lids drooped. Katie slowly withdrew the bottle, sensing that she might be full. The baby gazed up at her with sleepy eyes and smiled.

The fond, trusting smile melted Katie's heart. "You're safe now, little baby," she whispered, stroking the baby's feathery soft hair. "I'll make sure you're safe."

As if she understood Katie's meaning, the baby turned, nuzzled her face into Katie's arm, and fell asleep.

"Who would leave a baby like this?" Katie wondered, growing angry at the irresponsible parents. How could they just go away and leave her behind?

She stroked the baby's warm, peachy smooth cheek with the backs of her fingers. *Well, maybe they didn't mean to leave her*, Katie considered, softening. *Maybe something happened to them.*

"Something happened to them," she murmured, echoing out loud her silent thought. Just like something had happened to her own parents.

Katie rested her head back against the rock and let her mind wander. She remembered other autumns when her parents were still alive. She saw herself plowing joyfully through the vivid yellow, red, and orange leaves in Central Park. Her parents strolling a few paces behind, holding hands and smiling. The wide sky alive with crystal blue.

The memory had the quality of a dream, as if it had happened to someone else, some other girl who looked like Katie. It was becoming harder and harder to remember her parents. Their faces were growing hazy, out of focus.

She struggled to sharpen the image of her parents' faces, but couldn't.

Katie sat forward and remembered her locket sitting somewhere under the waterfall. If she still had it, all she'd have to do was open the locket to recall her parents faces exactly.

This baby's parents had better come back soon. Otherwise Katie would never be able to go back and look for the locket. Who knew where it would drift by tomorrow? Or even by now?

Soft, purring snores came from the baby. Her tiny round chest heaved up and down peacefully. Katie knelt forward, then rose to stand.

This was crazy.

She had to get her locket. She had to get home. It was growing darker by the minute. Once the light was completely gone, she'd never find her way out of the woods. She couldn't stand here holding some strange baby in her arms forever.

But she couldn't just walk off with someone's baby, either.

Yes, she could. She had to. Because there was no other choice. The deeply colored shadows were quickly converging into one uniform mantle of gray. And soon it would be pitch black. Not even moonlight would make it through the dense canopy of trees overhead.

Katie reached into the brown grocery bag and withdrew the plastic flashlight. Switching it on, she swung its thin, pale beam in all directions. The soft whiteness of the birch bark gave her an idea.

Katie settled the sleeping baby on the ground near the boulder, then peeled a foot-wide patch of bark from the nearest white birch tree. She picked up a short, thick stick and stirred it in the ashes of the dead fire. She held the birch bark flat with one hand while she used her other hand to write on the bark with her sooty stick.

I have your baby. She's safe. Don't worry. Call Katie at 555-5130.

Katie took the birch-bark message and propped it on the ground against the boulder. She rolled up the grocery bag and put it under her arm. Kneeling down, she scooped up the baby, who stirred and waved her arms in the air, but then settled down to sleep again.

Off in the distance, Katie could hear the rushing of the two waterfalls and the swirling pool. It was too late to look for her locket now, and way too dark.

With her flashlight beam cutting a pale yellow path

through the darkening woods, Katie walked with the baby in her arms. Even with the flashlight it was hard to see more than a few feet in front of her.

Follow the creek, she advised herself. No matter how dark it got, she'd be able to hear it. It wouldn't get her all the way back to the ranch, but at least she'd know she wasn't going in the wrong direction, deeper and deeper into the woods.

Her flashlight pointed toward the sound of the creek, Katie headed toward it. The baby snuffled and turned in her arms each time Katie stumbled over a rock or a fallen branch. In her sleep, the baby's tiny hand clutched the sleeve of Katie's jacket.

In a few minutes, the sound of the creek grew louder. Katie swept her flashlight beam along its swiftly moving waters.

So far so good, thought Katie, walking along the bank of the creek. She wondered whether Mel would look for her if she didn't come home. Probably not. Most likely he'd come home late and assume she was asleep. Ashley and Christina would think she'd just gone home. If she and the baby got lost out here in the woods, they'd be lost all night. No one would come looking for them.

Somewhere close by, a branch snapped. Katie looked around sharply but didn't see anything. *It was just an animal*, she reassured herself. Off in the distance something howled.

Katie clutched the baby tighter.

After a while, Katie began to worry. It felt like she'd been walking for too long. Could she have become confused and gone off the wrong way, following the creek that fed the second waterfall at the pool? It was possible.

Overhead an owl screamed as it dove for its prey.

Startled, Katie stumbled.

Her ankle turned painfully beneath her and she splashed into the creek, struggling to keep her balance. "No!" Katie shouted as the baby began to slip from her arms, howling in fright.

Katie clutched frantically at the falling baby. Just in time, she got hold. "Gotcha!" she cried out. The baby still yowled in terror, twisting in Katie's trembling arms.

At once, Katie realized she'd dropped her flashlight. Looking down, she saw it underwater a foot or so away, flashing crazily on and off, illuminating the water and rocks in short bursts of light.

Then it flashed off for good.

Katie held tightly to the screaming, squirming baby, as she stood helplessly engulfed in total darkness.

8

How could Katie keep the baby calm when her own heart was racing a mile a minute?

The baby's howls had died down to frightened sobs. Katie held her tight as she took the smallest possible steps in the jet blackness. Slowly and carefully, she made her way out of the creek and back onto the bank.

It was as though everything had disappeared—the trees, the rocks, the sky above.

I can't just stand here, Katie thought desperately. *I've got to keep moving.* Cautiously, she placed one foot in front of the other and began to move forward.

She was back in the pine forest and the scratchy needles made her heart jump every time they brushed her cheek. Now and then a branch snapped. Something scurried by. A strange yowl swept through the woods.

Her only comfort—her one guide—was the constant sound of the rushing creek. It was to her left and she could gauge her distance from it by the volume of its steady flow.

As she moved with tiny, painstaking steps, Katie started thinking of the creek as a friend. Its burbling rush took on the sound of a soothing song. *Keep on. Steady on. The morning will come, the morning will come, will come, will come.*

Katie closed her eyes and realized she was exhausted. She continued on with her eyes shut. It made no difference whether she opened or closed them. Either way, she was in complete darkness.

The baby's cries died down to a whimper.

Katie stopped, her eyes still closed. She couldn't keep going. What was the sense of it, anyway? She'd never find her way out of here tonight.

But it was getting colder. Her denim jacket wasn't enough anymore.

The baby must be freezing. All she had on was her little terrycloth stretchy suit. Katie couldn't believe how thoughtless she'd been. She had to wrap the baby in her jacket.

Katie opened her eyes.

A spot of bright light danced in front of her off in the distance.

She blinked hard. The light still shone before her. What was it? Was someone looking for her?

Katie struggled to get out of her jacket while keeping

hold of the baby, then wrapped the jacket around her. "Help!" she yelled. "I'm here! Help!"

The sound of Katie's shouting frightened the baby and she started crying again.

The light kept flickering in the distance, but it didn't come closer.

Katie thought hard and fast. It seemed to her that the light was in the same direction as the flow of the creek. Frantic that the light might disappear, Katie inched her way toward the creek. Then she stepped right into the icy water. Walking in the creek was the fastest way to get to the light. There was no chance of wandering off course.

She slogged through the water unsteadily. The baby cried and Katie bounced her lightly in what she hoped was a soothing motion. She tried hard to block out the crying, not to let it unnerve her.

It was still slow going, but with the distant light as her beacon, Katie had new hope.

What can that light be? she wondered. It swayed and flickered, but didn't move around too much.

It took ten long minutes until Katie got close enough to see where the light was coming from. "The bridge!" she gasped. The light was coming from the Angels Crossing Bridge!

Katie moved as quickly as she could to the shore. She could see the covered bridge pretty well now and no longer needed to stay in the creek. In fact, as she got closer to the bridge where the creek widened and the trees parted some, moonlight danced on the water. But it wasn't moonlight she'd seen. It was a much brighter light coming directly from the bridge.

When Katie was only yards from the bridge, she saw the source of the light. It came from a lantern hanging on a crossbeam in the center of the bridge's roof. Its strong warm light shone from within, casting the frame of the bridge into a black silhouette edged with ribbons of silver moonlight.

Three tall figures moved busily about on the bridge. Katie recognized them immediately.

"Ned! Edwina! Norma!" she shouted to them as she made her way ever more rapidly along the water's edge. "It's me! Katie! I need help!"

The three figures rushed to the side of the bridge and looked over. "Oh, good heavens!" cried Edwina, a beautiful blonde woman with long, soft, flowing curls. "It *is* Katie!"

The other woman's veil of straight black hair fell forward as she leaned further out over the side of the bridge. "Wait right there," Norma called down to Katie.

Katie wanted to sob with relief and happiness. The baby seemed to sense her change of mood and stopped crying. "It's okay, baby-baby," she told the warm little creature in her arms. "We made it."

In seconds, Norma was by her side. Katie looked up into Norma's serious face with its long, straight nose and high cheekbones. Norma's strange violet blue eyes—the same eyes as Ned's and Edwina's—focused on the baby. "How sweet," she murmured, as she took the baby from Katie and cradled her in her strong arms.

Katie expected Norma to ask what she was doing there in the woods in the middle of the night, but she didn't. The thought didn't even seem to enter her mind. Instead, she hummed to the baby swaddled in Katie's jacket, coaxing a bright smile from the tiny bewildered face.

Studying Norma's angular, dignified face in the lantern light, Katie wondered once again about this strange threesome. Part of her knew Norma was an angel. So were Edwina and Ned. Yet, another part of her still couldn't believe it. It was too . . . too unbelievable.

Norma wore a sleeveless T-shirt under denim coveralls. Her right cheek was smeared with dirt. Looking at her, Katie couldn't believe she was really an angel. There was no hint of a wing or a shimmering robe or a halo or anything anywhere.

"Come on," Norma told Katie, calmly walking back toward the bridge.

Katie followed her as quickly as she could, feeling the weight of her heavy wet work boots and soaked jeans. On the bridge, she saw the large, old-fashioned lantern again. Ned and Edwina seemed to shine under its light. Yet, despite the brilliant glow from above, there was nothing angelic about them, either.

Ned was a pleasant-faced young man with sandy-blond hair. He was dressed in jeans and a flannel shirt. Edwina had a model's kind of breathtaking beauty that needed no makeup or fancy clothing. She, too, was dressed simply in faded blue jeans and a white T-shirt.

All three had two things in common. One thing was height. Norma, Ned, and Edwina were all over six-feet tall. The other trait they shared was their amazing violet blue eyes.

Edwina rushed to Katie's side. "You're shivering!" she cried, her musical voice filled with concern. "Your clothes are so damp."

Katie took a step forward and her blue-jeaned legs brushed together wetly. She shivered, reminded of how cold she really was.

It suddenly occurred to Katie that Ned, Norma, and Edwina seemed totally unaware of the chill in the air. Norma's sleeveless T-shirt couldn't be keeping her warm. Neither could Edwina nor Ned's clothes, really, not without jackets. And none of them wore shoes! "Aren't you cold?" she asked impulsively.

Ned shrugged. "We don't like to wear heavy clothes when we're cleaning."

"Cleaning?" Katie questioned.

"Sure," Ned said, nodding at a pile of sponges, mops, and suds-filled buckets Katie hadn't noticed before on the bridge. "Somebody's got to do it."

"I guess," Katie murmured, not really knowing *what* to say. Somehow she never thought of angels as *cleaning* things, but, of course, she never thought of angels as being anything like Ned, Norma, and Edwina.

And, as usual, now that she was face to face with them, she found it hard to accept that they really were angels at all.

Suddenly, Katie became aware that something had changed. She looked down and saw her boots were completely dry, and so were her jeans. She was no longer shivering. How had *that* happened? She looked up, startled.

Edwina patted her shoulder.

Ned grinned and glanced up at the lantern. "This lantern throws a lot of heat. It's a terrific lantern."

Was that supposed to be an explanation? Katie wondered. Norma, Ned, and Edwina were always friendly and nice, but Katie was nervous around them.

She was distracted from her thoughts by the sound of the baby's crying.

"Poor thing is hungry," Norma crooned, still cradling the baby fondly in her arms. She scooped up a silver thermos on the floor and unscrewed the top. From the pocket of her coveralls, she produced a bottle, exactly the same kind of bottle Katie had found with the baby.

"Wow!" Katie gasped. "Where did you get that?"

Norma, who usually wore a serious expression, smiled slightly and nodded at a soggy brown grocery bag in the corner. "In the bag. I found it floating in the creek," she said. "Things tend to flow to where they need to be."

Turning back to her thermos, Norma poured some of its milky contents into the bottle.

"What are you giving her?" Katie asked. "You don't have baby formula in there, do you?"

"Oh, of course not," Norma said as she gently fed the baby.

"I don't think babies are supposed to have regular milk until they're older," Katie warned, concerned for the infant. Norma might be an angel, but that didn't necessarily mean she knew about babies. At any rate, Katie didn't want to take any chances.

"This isn't regular milk," Norma assured her while the baby guzzled contentedly. "But it's the best thing in the world for babies. Trust me. It's exactly what she needs."

Katie came close to Norma and examined the bottle. The fluid inside was a watery cream color seemingly infused with tiny, sparkling lights. "Are you sure?" she asked uncertainly.

"Absolutely," Norma replied with confidence.

The baby liked whatever it was, that much was certain. She seemed blissfully happy there in Norma's arms.

A pang of jealousy stabbed Katie. "I'll hold her," she said, reaching out for the baby. "I think she's more used to me."

"Here you go," Norma said as she handed the baby over to Katie. "What's her name?"

"I don't know. I found her in the woods."

"Well, you have to call her something," said Edwina, who had gone back to scrubbing the bridge floor with a thick-bristled scrubbing brush. "How about Fern?"

"Fern?" Ned questioned. "Why?"

"It sounds pretty, and ferns are things you find in the woods," Edwina said as if it should have been obvious. "It's certainly better than calling her pine or moss or boulder or birch or creek or—"

"Creek's not bad," Ned offered.

"No, creek's a terrible name for a baby," Norma disagreed.

"Fern," Katie repeated. "That's good." She gazed down at the baby. "Hi, Fern."

She wondered why the three of them weren't more curious about where this baby came from. But, since they were angels, maybe they already knew.

If they knew, then perhaps they could tell her where the parents were. "Don't you think it was strange that this baby was just sitting there all alone in the woods?" she began.

"Extremely strange," Edwina agreed, still scrubbing.

"Do you know who her parents are?" Katie asked bluntly.

Ned looked to Norma and Norma looked to Edwina for a possible answer. "No. Do you?" Edwina asked Katie.

Katie shook her head. "I was hoping *you* did."

The three of them shook their heads at the same time. *Some angels*, Katie thought. When the baby had finished the bottle, she tossed uncomfortably in Katie's arms. "What's the matter?" Katie asked, feeling helpless.

"Hold her up and pat her back," Norma advised.

Katie tried it and in moments the baby burped loudly. Everyone laughed and the baby settled her head on Katie's shoulder. Her tiny arm wrapped itself around Katie's neck, her chubby hand soft and warm.

Would you like me to walk you back to the ranch?" Ned offered.

"Oh, sure," Edwina teased. "Anything to get out of cleaning."

"I'll be right back," Ned said as he leapt onto the side rail of the bridge with a dancer's fluid grace and reached up to unhook the lantern. He jumped down, holding the lamp up in front of him. "Come on, Katie."

"Take this," Norma said, offering Katie the silver thermos.

"Thanks. Bye," Katie said to Edwina and Norma. "Oh, by the way, if you see a silver locket floating by, it's mine. This pesty, weird crow stole it from me and dropped it. I'd sure love to have it back. It means a lot to me."

Norma nodded. "Things tend to flow to where they need to be," she said for the second time.

That wasn't what Katie wanted to hear. She wanted her locket back. "Well, if you see it, grab it, would you?"

"Will do," Edwina assured her with a smile.

Katie nodded at them and waved. She and Ned walked through the woods without speaking. The bright lantern light blazed a path for them as they climbed the hill leading away from the bridge. On the way up, they startled a raccoon that scampered out of their way.

With the light, the woods didn't seem frightening at all. But suddenly, at the top of the hill, Katie realized something. "You left Edwina and Norma in the dark," she told Ned, recalling how utterly dark the woods had been without her flashlight.

"They'll be all right," he said, unconcerned.

Katie looked back over her shoulder. In the dark, she could barely see the bridge itself, but moving across it, back and forth, were two gorgeous winged angels, ablaze with a dazzling white light.

9

Katie couldn't tear herself away from the glorious, angelic image on the bridge. Hugging the slumbering Fern, she stared at the winged angels glowing so brightly, trying to memorize the sight of them so that they'd be forever real to her.

But she was also aware of Ned's rapid footsteps moving quickly and steadily through the woods ahead of her.

Katie didn't want to be left behind in the dark woods. The way Edwina, Ned, and Norma came and went, who knew where they'd be in the next second?

She forced herself to turn away from the angel vision, but it was hard. With one last awe-filled look over her shoulder, she ran to catch up with Ned, holding Fern tightly and trying not to awaken her.

"You guys really *are* angels, aren't you?" she said

breathlessly when she caught up to him.

Ned looked at her and smiled, his face aglow in the lantern light. "You've met more of us than you even know," he said.

"I have?" Katie questioned. "Like when?"

Fern stirred in her arms and whimpered softly. Her dark eyes blinked, then closed.

"Shhh," Ned said, putting his finger to his lip. "We don't want to wake her."

He continued walking, the lantern light guiding the way, and it seemed he went even more quickly than before. Katie had to hurry to keep up with him.

She wanted to know when she'd met angels without realizing she had, but their pace was too brisk for conversation. *Is he deliberately going fast to avoid telling me?* Katie wondered. She was determined to find out, though. "When?" she panted behind him. "What other angels have I seen?"

Ned stopped a moment to let Katie catch up. His expression was resigned, as if he'd decided to stop avoiding the question. "If you think hard, you'll start to realize who the angels were."

"No, tell me," Katie pleaded.

"The police officer you met today."

"No!" Katie gasped.

Ned nodded. "Please stay inside the truck and use your seat belt in the future."

"Was that you?" Katie gasped.

"No. There are lots of us. We talk."

"What other angels have I met?"

"The woman who came to your friend's apartment that day."

Katie's jaw dropped in astonishment. She knew exactly who he was talking about, although she'd completely forgotten about the woman until that very moment.

Before the police came to Addy's apartment to tell them about Katie's parents' car crash, Katie had climbed out onto the fire escape. Addy was taking a shower and Katie was bored with waiting for her. Katie often liked to stand on the fire escape and watch life go on around her in the street down below.

That day she'd been startled by a dark-haired woman in a soft red-and-purple flowered dress who came climbing, barefoot, down from the fire escape above her. "It's a beautiful world, isn't it?" she'd said to Katie as she looked out over the rooftops.

Katie had agreed. It was a drizzly day, but the rooftops and windows glistened and the sky looked as if it was about to clear.

"No matter what happens to you, there are forces in the world that will support you," the woman said with an unexpected intensity. "If you believe in the goodness of the world, it will be there for you. Even in hard times." The woman looked at Katie with piercing green eyes. Katie felt uncomfortable under her scrutiny, yet she couldn't look away. She felt strangely drawn to the woman. "You are a beautiful girl," the woman said. "Be strong. Many people will love you."

Katie wasn't frightened of the woman. The city was full of odd people who said strange philosophical things. Some of them were scary, some were insane, but this woman wasn't. At least she didn't seem so to Katie. The woman put her hand on Katie's arm. Her touch was warm and feather-light.

At that moment, Addy's mother called to her from inside the apartment. There was something so urgent in her voice, Katie instantly said good-bye to the woman and scrambled back through the window.

"*She* was an angel?" Katie now said wonderingly.

Ned nodded.

Although Katie had forgotten the woman, she remembered that at the moment she got the news that her parents were dead, she'd staggered backward and closed her eyes. Strangely, the image of that woman's face had formed behind her eyelids. In those first few pain-filled hours, Katie had envisioned that face whenever she shut her eyes. In some inexplicable way, it had helped her make it through.

Before long, Katie and Ned neared the ranch. Katie saw the lights of Ashley's ranch-style house, Christina's cabin, and the outdoor lights from the stable on the other side of the trees. They looked so warm and inviting.

"Home again," Ned said, lifting his lantern a bit higher. The lantern threw a bright ribbon of light down the trampled dirt horse path that would lead Katie the rest of the way out of the woods.

Katie squeezed the still-slumbering baby and smiled up at Ned. She felt so happy and safe with him. He seemed so human and real. He seemed like the nicest person in the world. Not some unearthly, mysterious angel.

Gazing fondly down at Fern, Katie stroked her cheek. "What should I do with this baby, Ned?" she asked. "You're an angel. Tell me what to do."

"Don't drop that thermos."

Katie glanced at the silver thermos she held in her hand. "No, I mean what do I do with Fern?"

Ned didn't answer. Katie turned to him—but he was gone.

"Ned?" Katie turned in a circle looking for him.

The horse path was still illuminated, but where was Ned with his lantern? Katie looked up and saw that the light from an immense orange moon had blazed its way through the treetops, here where the pines were a little less dense.

She followed the path back to the ranch. But when she got to the stable, she hesitated. What would Mr. and Mrs. Kingsley do if she appeared on their doorstep holding a strange baby? Katie needed time to think about it. She didn't even know how late it was.

Keeping to the shadows, Katie circled until she came to the back of Ashley's house. Her long legs made it easy for her to climb over the rail fence that separated the backyard from the woods. She knew Ashley's bedroom window was right there on the corner, but the light was off. Was Ashley asleep?

Katie held the baby tight and sneaked to the window. "Ashley!" she whispered sharply as she rapped lightly on the window. "Ashley!"

A small light snapped on, and Katie saw Ashley sit up in bed, sleepy-eyed. "Ashley!" Katie whispered more loudly, rapping gently again.

Ashley's eyes shifted slowly to the window, then went wide with surprise. Throwing off her green flowered comforter, she dashed to the window, her red flannel nightgown flowing behind her. "Katie! What on earth . . . I thought you went home! What have you got there?" she spoke excitedly as she opened the window.

Katie carefully climbed in over Ashley's desk, trying not to jostle the baby.

"Katie! That's a baby!" Ashley gasped.

"I know."

Ashley leaned over the baby. "Oh, it's so *cute!*" Then she jumped back. "Where did you get it?"

"In the woods."

"What's going on?" Ashley demanded, her hands anxiously pushing back her disheveled curls. "Are you all right?"

Holding the baby, Katie sat on Ashley's bed. "I'm all right *now*, thanks to Ned, Norma, and Edwina."

Ashley's hands flew to her face. "You saw them again?" she cried, rushing to Katie's side. "Tell me. Tell me everything."

Katie told her all that had happened—how she'd lost her locket, found the baby, been lost in the dark, and found by the angels. She told of seeing Edwina and Norma in their celestial forms there on the bridge and how Ned had disappeared so suddenly.

"Wow!" Ashley murmured. "Wow."

The baby's eyes blinked open sleepily.

"I'm calling her Fern," Katie told Ashley.

"Fern. That's pretty. What's in the *Star Trek* thermos?"

"*Star Trek* what?" Katie looked down at the silver thermos. Only, it wasn't silver anymore. It was a blue plastic thermos with all the characters from *Star Trek*, both new and old versions, pictured on it. "This used to be silver!" she gasped.

"Well, it's plastic now," Ashley commented.

"Wait until you see the weird stuff that's in it. It *sparkles*." Laying the baby gently on the bed, Katie unscrewed the top. "Look at this," she said, handing the thermos to Ashley.

Ashley gazed down into the thermos. "*I* don't see any sparkles," she told Katie.

Katie grabbed it back and looked inside. Ashley was right. No sparkles. She sniffed the thermos. Baby formula. "It *did* sparkle. And it *was* silver," she insisted.

"I believe you," said Ashley. "Angels."

"What do you think I should do with her?" Katie asked.

"I think you should call the police," Ashley said uncertainly.

"The police?" Katie yelped. "No way! Why call them?"

"I think that's what you're supposed to do when you find a baby," Ashley insisted.

"But the police will take her away," Katie cried.

"I guess so," Ashley agreed.

"Then what will they do, put her in an orphanage?" Katie demanded.

"I don't know," Ashley admitted. "I don't think they have orphanages anymore. I suppose they'll give her to foster parents who'll take care of her."

"What if the foster parents are mean?" Katie asked, putting her hand protectively on Fern's pudgy leg. "I don't want anyone to take Fern away. Things flow to where they need to be and Fern flowed to me."

Ashley scowled at Katie as if she'd lost her mind. "What?"

"Well, sort of," Katie mumbled.

Fern squirmed on the bed and began to cry loudly. Ashley jumped up in alarm. "She's going to wake everyone. If my parents find her they *will* call the police."

Katie picked up Fern, but she kept crying. "I have to feed her. Oh, and I left the baby bottle on the bridge. How stupid! I left her bag behind, too."

Ashley ran to the door and opened it a crack. "My mother's coming!" she whispered in an alarmed hoarse whisper. "Do you want to let her know about the baby or not?"

"No!" Katie said decidedly as she ducked into Ashley's closet with Fern. Amazingly, as soon as they were inside the closet, Fern stopped crying. "Good girl," Katie whispered, rocking her soothingly.

In a minute, Katie heard Mrs. Kingsley. "Ashley are you all right? I heard a strange sound, like a baby crying."

"Oh, no," Ashley replied in a voice which sounded strained and false to Katie. "I . . . I woke up and couldn't go back to sleep, so I turned on the radio. It came on really loud and I shut it off again."

"Why can't you sleep?"

"I don't know. Maybe the light from the full moon was bothering me."

Katie heard Mrs. Kingsley enter the room and pull down the shade. "It's some moon tonight," she commented. "They call it a harvest moon. Or is it a hunter's moon? I'm never sure. It's very big and golden, though."

"That's better," Ashley said.

"Are you sure everything is all right?" Mrs. Kingsley asked.

"Sure. Fine. Really, Mom," Ashley said hastily.

"Try to sleep then."

The bedroom door shut, and Ashley tapped on the closet door. "Coast is clear."

Katie came out into the bedroom with Fern. "Good thing she didn't cry."

Ashley studied Fern quizzically. "Yeah, it was almost like she knew to keep quiet."

Fern grunted and began to twist in Katie's arms. "She's still hungry, though," said Katie. She was already getting familiar with Fern's signals. "She's going to cry again soon."

Ashley cast a worried glance at her bedroom door. "Maybe we should just tell my parents, Katie. You can't keep her."

"Why not?"

"Because you can't."

Katie turned her back on Ashley and jiggled the whimpering baby in her arms. She couldn't just give Fern to strangers. She was responsible for her. She'd saved her life. They'd struggled through the dark woods together.

When she looked at Fern's little face, her heart moved. Actually moved. That's how it felt, anyway.

Was that love? Katie didn't know.

But she did know she couldn't just hand Fern over to anyone until she was sure beyond the slightest doubt that it was the right thing to do.

"I have to think about it," she told Ashley stubbornly.

Fern yipped loudly, her face reddening.

Ashley wrung her hands. "Well, you'd better think fast!"

10

"Wait up. I keep tripping on my nightgown," Ashley complained as she trailed behind Katie. As Fern's whimpers turned into cries, Katie had taken Fern and ducked out the window to avoid being heard. Ashley had pulled on a robe and gone out after her.

Now they hurried through the pine woods behind Ashley's house. "I know, we can go to Christina's house," said Katie.

"Then Alice will hear Fern," Ashley disagreed. "No. Wait! She won't. Alice might not be home yet. She had a date tonight."

"What time is it, anyway?" Katie asked, rocking Fern back and forth trying to quiet her sobs.

"Around ten-thirty."

"Did Mel call looking for me?"

"Uh-uh," Ashley told her.

"What a concerned guy," Katie said scornfully. She didn't really expect Mel to come looking for her, but it would have been nice, just the same. "Okay," she said, "let's go to Christina's."

They ran along the edge of the woods until they came to the back of Christina's house. Ashley checked to see if Alice's truck was there, but saw no sign of it. Lights were on inside the house, though. They hurried around to the front and banged on Christina's door. Inside, Katie heard the murmuring sounds of a TV. "Good, she's awake," she told Ashley.

In minutes, Christina answered, dressed in a nightshirt printed all over with lots of small rainbows. "What's going on?" she asked as she held the door open for them to hurry through. "What's that? Oh, my gosh! It's a baby!"

"We know," Ashley and Katie said at the same time.

Fern began to wail at full volume.

Christina cupped her chin with her hands and started hopping nervously around the living room. "This is too unbelievable. *Too* unbelievable. This is freaky. Totally freaky."

"Chill, would you," Katie scolded. "Haven't you ever heard a baby cry?"

"No, no. That's not what's freaky," Christina said, reaching behind a dark green armchair. "Look what I have." She held up a rumpled brown grocery bag. "You won't believe what's inside it."

"Baby clothes, a pacifier, a bottle, and a rag doll," Katie said in an amazed voice.

Ashley and Christina stared at Katie, dumbstruck.

"Where did you get it?" Katie asked.

"Champ found it in back of the barn," Christina said. Champ was Ashley's golden retriever. "He picked it up and brought it to me. I thought maybe one of the riders left it. How did you know what was in it, Katie?"

"I found it with Fern, but I dropped it when I fell in the creek. Then Norma found it, but I left it behind by mistake and—"

"Norma found it?" Christina interrupted. "What's happened?"

Katie quickly recapped the day's events for Christina while she washed out the baby bottle and filled it with fresh formula. She looked hard at the formula, trying to detect even the slightest sparkle, but it looked like plain, ordinary baby formula. *Strange*, she thought, shaking her head. As soon as Katie sat on the couch and put the bottle to Fern's lips, the baby stopped howling.

"You left the bag on the bridge, and then *I* found the bag," Christina murmured as Katie concluded her story. She leaned back against the kitchen counter, staring in wonder at the baby. "Wow! Maybe the angels brought it to the edge of the woods."

"Could be," Ashley agreed, taking a seat on the couch beside Katie.

"And you know what else is strange?" Katie said. "This thermos doesn't seem to be getting any emptier. I mean, each time there's a little bit less, but I can never seem to get to the end of it."

Christina raised her eyebrows significantly. Katie could see the little scar above her left eye wrinkle.

"Wow," Ashley breathed.

Their silent speculation was abruptly ended as Katie felt something warm and wet on her arm. She jumped up. "Oh, no! I need a new diaper!"

The girls looked at one another, wide-eyed. "Where are we going to get a diaper?" Ashley asked.

"Get something!" said Katie, holding out her soaked arm.

A sweet, high-pitched giggle came from Fern. The girls all stared at her, shocked.

"She thinks it's funny," Christina said, amazed.

"She does," Ashley agreed, smiling.

Fern chortled this time, her face gleeful.

"What a little comedian," Katie giggled. "Very funny, Fern." She looked at Christina and Ashley. "I still need a diaper."

"A towel," Christina said, rushing to the kitchen. She grabbed a clean kitchen towel from a drawer. "This will do for now."

The girls laid Fern on the couch and took off her soaked cotton diaper. Using the pins from the old diaper, they put the towel around her bottom, then changed her into the new stretchy suit from the grocery bag. Katie held up the white stretchy with pink rosebuds printed all over it. "Considering what this bag has been through, the stuff inside is in great shape," she commented.

When Fern had been wriggled into her new outfit, Christina handed her the rag doll from the bag. Fern cooed to the doll and rubbed it against her cheek. "Oh, she's so cute," sighed Christina, gazing fondly at Fern. "What are you going to do with her?"

"Katie wants to keep her," Ashley told Christina.

"Keep her?" Christina cried. "You can't do that!"

"I just want to keep her until I think about it some more," Katie insisted. "Look at her. If we hand her over to the police, she'll spend the night in some strange place where she doesn't know anyone. She'll be scared."

"*This* is a strange place to her," Ashley pointed out. "Anywhere she goes will be a strange place."

"But Fern knows me now," Katie argued. "It's bad enough that her mother is gone. If I leave, too, she might get . . . you know . . . traumatized."

"What will Mel do if he sees her?" Christina asked.

"Who knows?" Katie said scornfully. "I'd better call him." Using the kitchen phone, Katie called home. The phone rang and rang. "Either he's asleep or he didn't come home," Katie reported as she hung up. "Obviously, he's not too worried."

"Maybe he's out looking for you," Christina suggested.

Katie's raised her eyebrows skeptically. "Mel?"

"You're right," Christina agreed. "He's probably asleep."

"Hey!" Katie cried as she thought of an idea. "Could I sneak into an empty room in the guest house?"

"There's no one there," Ashley said. "The whole place is empty. The last employee left today. Dad's going to board the house up for the season, but he hasn't gotten to it yet."

"Perfect," said Katie. "No one will even know Fern and I are there."

Christina frowned. "What if Fern's parents are looking for her?"

"We'll try to find them in the morning, okay?"

"Okay," Christina and Ashley agreed, reluctantly.

"But, you know what," Katie added. "I think Fern's been abandoned."

"Really?" said Christina. "Why?"

"I waited a long time in those woods, and no one came back."

"Maybe her mother got hurt and couldn't come back," Ashley said.

"Maybe," Katie agreed. "But I just have a feeling she dumped Fern."

"Who would go away and leave such a darling baby?" Christina asked.

"It happens," Katie said knowingly. "Kids get left alone in the world all the time."

11

That night, Katie snuggled close to baby Fern. The heavy red-and-black checked woolen blankets she found in the guest house closet kept them both pretty warm, but outside a cold wind rattled the windows. The plain, rustic guest house was cooler than Katie liked. She pulled Fern close to her in the twin bed in case she, too, was cold.

Fern awoke once during the night and her hungry cries awakened Katie. The huge autumn moon shone in the window, casting a golden glow over the pine dresser, wooden floor, and simple straightback chair in the bedroom. Looking out, Katie saw that the moon had risen higher in the sky and lost some of its intense orange color, but it was still huge and mysterious looking.

Fern howled and Katie crossed her fingers that she

was simply hungry. She grabbed the bottle from the floor and fed Fern, who instantly settled down to drink it. She wondered about the baby formula as she lay there with Fern in the crook of her arm, contentedly sucking from the bottle. Were those twinkling lights she'd seen still there in the formula, somehow mysteriously masked by a more ordinary appearance? Was the thermos still silver beneath its mask of ordinary plastic?

Were people really more silvery, sparkly on some other mysterious level than they appeared to be in everyday life?

Fern fell back to sleep, and Katie gently removed the bottle from her lips. In minutes, her eyes closed, too.

In what seemed like only a moment later, Katie's eyes snapped open. Only it was more than a moment. The stream of sunshine pouring through the window told her that much.

Something banged. The sound came from the living room just down the hall from Katie's first-floor bedroom. It was the front door. Katie quickly sat up. Who was coming?

Scooping Fern out of bed, Katie hurried into the closet. Fern whimpered and Katie put her hand over her mouth. "Shhhh." As she held Fern, Katie quickly realized that the baby was soaking wet. Her towel diaper had soaked through to her stretchy suit.

"Katie? Katie?"

It was Ashley. Katie's shoulders sagged with relief as

she came out of the closet. "You scared me," she said ruefully.

"Sorry," said Ashley as she threw two plastic bags on the bed and removed a canvas backpack from her shoulders. "Christina and I rode our bikes to town early this morning and got a few things for Fern."

Sitting Fern on the bed, Katie looked in the plastic bags and found a package of disposable diapers, baby wipes, jars of organically grown baby food and box of the same brand of cereal, a can of baby formula, and a buttered roll in a wax-paper bag. "The roll is for you," Ashley said.

"Thanks," said Katie, tearing open the disposable diapers. "Where's Christina?"

"She went to call for Molly so she can help us look for the baby's parents today."

"Molly? I don't want a lot of people to know about this, Ashley."

"I know, I know," Ashley said, "but Christina wanted to tell Molly. She thought it would be better to have more people searching. And you know Christina's intuition is usually pretty on-target."

"I suppose, but no one else should find out," Katie agreed grudgingly as she pulled Fern's clothing off and removed the wet towel. She wiped the baby down with the baby wipes and put a disposable diaper on her. "There, that's better."

Ashley pulled Fern's pink stretchy suit from her backpack. "Here, I washed this last night," she said, handing it to Katie. "Oh, and Mel called. I told him you were on a trail ride, but that you'd slept over and were going to sleep over again tonight since we don't have school tomorrow. He seemed cool with that."

"Great," said Katie, wriggling Fern into the outfit.

Ashley sat on the bed beside Katie. "You won't believe what we heard at O'Herlihy's market," she said. "Mr. O'Herlihy told us about some young redheaded woman who came into the store two days ago asking for organic baby food. He said she was all dirty and scruffy like she'd been living in the woods or something."

"Living in the woods! That must be Fern's mother!" Katie cried excitedly, then she frowned. "Why did he tell you about her? Do you think he was suspicious?" she asked, snapping Fern's outfit.

"No. He mentioned it because we bought this organic baby food stuff. He didn't know if he should sell it to us since he'd ordered it for her. But she hadn't come back for it, so he let us buy it."

"She didn't come back for it, huh," Katie said thoughtfully. She tried to keep her expression serious and concerned, but inside she was smiling. She loved Fern. It didn't seem possible to love someone in just one day, but that was how she felt. She didn't want to give her back, especially not to some irresponsible mother who had left her all alone in the woods.

Christina and Molly came in just then. "What a cute baby!" Molly cried. She rushed to the bed and playfully dangled the end of her long, white-blonde braid in front of the baby.

Fern screwed her face into an unhappy knot and howled, fat tears springing to her dark eyes.

Katie gathered her up protectively. "She's not a kitten," she scolded Molly.

"Well, I've never been around babies," Molly defended herself huffily.

"Maybe she wants some food," Ashley suggested.

Fern gobbled the baby peaches that Katie fed her straight from the jar with a plastic spoon. She looked so cute with her face full of peach mush.

"I was thinking about this parent search," Molly said as Katie wiped Fern's smiling face. "The first thing we should do is search the woods."

"I agree," Christina said. "What if the mother has broken her leg and is lying out there in unspeakable pain?"

"What if right now she's on a train to Florida or somewhere?" Katie countered. "And if there's a father, where's he? Did he break his leg, too? It's not likely both of them did. Face it, Fern's mother has probably skipped out on her."

"We should at least look," Ashley said reasonably.

"We should," Christina agreed. "I wish I knew Fern's exact date of birth. I'd do an astrological chart for her. Last night I even laid out the tarot and tried to pick cards for Fern, but Fern really has to pick her own cards or I don't think it's valid."

"Yes, Fern will have to be at least two before you can map her destiny," Katie said sarcastically.

"I was just trying to help," Christina defended herself.

"Come on," Katie said, dumping the pillow out of its flannel pillowcase so she could wrap Fern in it. "Let's go search and get it over with."

The girls spent the entire morning in the woods, calling out for Fern's mother. "Hello! Anybody there? Hello?" Katie led the others along the creek, trying to find her way back to the campsite. She also hoped to get back to the swirling pool and look for her lost locket.

They walked for nearly a half hour but saw no sign of the pool or the birch forest. "The creek must branch off in some strange way we didn't notice," Katie said, shifting Fern in her arms. "We must be following the wrong branch of it."

They went back and tried to find a place where the stream split, but couldn't.

When they came to the Angels Crossing Bridge, it stood silent and empty. Molly stared at it, mesmerized. "That's where the angel told me I didn't have to starve myself into thinness to be lovable," she said quietly.

Katie looked at her. Molly was still very slim, but had lost the gaunt, unhealthy look she'd had just before she went into the hospital.

By the middle of the afternoon, the girls were ready to give up. "This is hopeless," Ashley admitted. She turned to Katie with a serious expression. "Katie, we're going to have to contact someone in authority. You can't just keep a baby. Even if you were an adult, you wouldn't be allowed to do that. But you're only a kid. You can't even really take care of a baby."

Katie held onto Fern as if Ashley were trying to take the baby away from her. "I can so take care of her."

"Not forever," Christina pointed out gently. "What about school?"

Katie shifted uneasily from side to side. "I don't know," she muttered without looking at any of them.

"Katie, you don't seriously want to keep Fern, do you?" Ashley asked gently.

"What if I do?" Katie challenged her. "Maybe Aunt Rainie and Uncle Jeff will adopt her."

"Your uncle complains about his bills all the time as it is," Ashley reminded her. "And if they had a baby, your aunt would have to stop working or hire a sitter. I don't know that they'd want a baby."

Katie hugged Fern tight. Fierce tears blurred her vision. "Well, I want her. I know how it feels to be a kid no one wants, and that's not going to happen to Fern. No way!"

12

Late that afternoon, the girls sat sprawled on two soft couches in front of a stone fireplace. They were in the main room of the vacant guest house eating a pizza Ashley had ordered. As they sat munching pizza, they tried to figure out what to do next.

Every now and then, one of them tossed out an idea. Molly suggested offering a cash reward to anyone who'd seen a person in the woods with a baby. Christina wanted them to all hold hands and meditate on the problem. Ashley suggested anonymously calling the department of social services and asking exactly what one did with a found baby.

None of the ideas seemed right, and the girls fell back into a silence broken only by the crack and fizz of a pop-top soda can being opened and by the sound of Katie sneezing loudly.

Katie had discovered that if she made a noise like sneezing, Fern dissolved into giggles that lit her sweet baby face in delight.

The chuckles were so irresistible that Katie faked sneeze after sneeze just for the joy of hearing Fern laugh as she kicked her feet in the air from the couch beside Katie.

"I love that sound," Molly said, tickling Fern under her soft chin. "She's so adorable when she laughs."

Fern smiled up at Molly, her eyes shining happily. "She *is* adorable, isn't she," Katie said fondly.

Katie realized she no longer felt the strong urge to claim Fern as hers alone. It was okay if Fern liked Molly because Katie now felt sure Fern loved her. She could tell from the way the baby looked at her with soft, glowing eyes, the way she rested her head on Katie's shoulder and wrapped her tiny, trusting hand around Katie's finger. In the course of this first real day together, she'd come to realize a special, strong bond had been formed between them.

"I have an idea," Ashley said, suddenly sitting forward. "Tomorrow is the big Pine Ridge Fire Department Halloween Picnic. There's always lots of free food, and it's easy to sneak into the picnic without even paying the admission fee."

"So?" Molly questioned.

"So, if the mother is still in the area, it might draw her out. She probably doesn't have much money and it would be a free meal," Ashley went on reasonably.

"We don't even know what she looks like," Molly objected. "Maybe it's a father."

"We know something about the mother because of what Mr. O'Herlihy said this morning," Christina pointed out. "Maybe there's also a father, but we definitely know there's a mother. It's got to be her. He said she looked scruffy, like she'd been living in the woods and she wanted organic baby food. He didn't say what she looked like, though, except that she had red hair."

"I'll go to O'Herlihy's and ask," Ashley said. "I'll say that . . . ummm . . . I know! That I'm doing a report on organic baby products! That that's why I bought them earlier, and I want to talk to the red-haired woman since she seemed to know something about them."

"What good will that do?" Katie asked. "She dumped Fern. She's not going to want her back."

"Maybe she *will* want her back if we talk to her. It will at least give us a chance to get a look at her," Molly said. "We'll be able to tell what sort of person she is."

"If she seems like a nice person maybe we *can* talk her into taking Fern back," Christina agreed. "You know, maybe she's just someone who's had some bad luck and given up hope."

"A person like that leaves their baby on a doorstep, not in the woods," Katie said scornfully. "What if I hadn't found her? What then?"

The girls looked at one another soberly.

Ashley put her hand on Katie's shoulder. "You saved her life, Katie. But you'd better face the fact that your aunt and uncle might not want to keep Fern. And if they don't—which they probably won't—you'll have to give her to *someone*. You can't keep her."

Katie set her jaw defiantly. She knew she couldn't keep Fern, but she didn't want to deal with that reality just yet. She needed more time to think. "You guys better go now. I want to feed Fern and give her a bath." She got to her feet with Fern in her arms. "I'm tired, too. I want to get to bed early."

"I still say the Halloween Picnic is worth a try," Ashley insisted as she picked up the empty pizza box from the floor. "While we're there we can ask the volunteer ambulance drivers if they took anyone to the hospital lately. They'd remember if it was a stranger because they know most of the regular people in Pine Ridge."

"Maybe the mother has amnesia!" Christina suggested.

"That only happens on TV," Molly disagreed.

"It must happen *sometimes* in real life," said Christina. "You never know."

"All right," Katie finally agreed. "We'll try the picnic tomorrow." In her heart, she didn't think it was a very good idea, but it would buy her some time until Uncle Jeff and Aunt Rainie got home. The more time that passed without anyone claiming Fern, the better her chances of keeping her, or at least of talking her aunt and uncle into it. "Let me feed and bathe her while there's still light," Katie said. "Once it's dark I don't want to attract attention by turning on any lights."

"Are you sure you'll be all right here by yourself tonight?" Christina asked.

"Yeah, sure," Katie said confidently. "This is the perfect place to hide out."

"Okay, see you in the morning," Ashley said, jamming the pizza box into a tall trash can.

After her friends left, Katie fed Fern. Once again the peach mush covered Fern's laughing face. Fern even delighted in rubbing some of it into her own soft, dark hair.

"Oh, Fern," Katie scolded with a smile. "You are a *total* mess."

In the guest house kitchen, Katie found a plastic basin that fit into the stainless steel sink. It looked perfect for bathing Fern.

When the bath was done, Katie diapered and dressed Fern. Carrying her to a window, she looked out at the brilliant orange and pink sunset.

Fern rested her head sleepily on Katie's shoulder. Her small fingers rested around Katie's neck. "Hi, hi, my angel pie," Katie began to sing as she swayed gently.

Katie watched the flaming sunset die down into a gentle blue-gray dusk. She felt happy and calm with Fern there so close and safe. Fern yawned and turned her face into Katie's shoulder. Katie rubbed her back. "I love you, Fern," she whispered.

In a few more minutes, Katie realized Fern had drifted off to sleep. Katie carried her to the bedroom and gently placed her under the covers. She propped a pillow alongside Fern to make sure she wouldn't roll out of bed, then pulled off her shoes and jeans and climbed into bed beside her. Stretching once before settling on her side, Katie snuggled into her pillow, exhausted from her day of searching the woods with a baby in her arms.

In the middle of the night, Katie was awakened by Fern's sharp cries. In the brilliant moonlight she saw the baby pitching from side to side as she screamed. "What's the matter?" she asked, scooping Fern from the bed.

Fern continued crying. "Does your tummy hurt?" Katie asked, rocking her. "Are you getting another tooth?"

Fern's shrieks seemed so pain-filled that Katie grew panicky. What if this was serious?

She got out of bed with Fern in her arms. The baby's cries died down to breathy sobs, then stopped altogether.

"Whew!" Katie sighed with relief, sitting back down on the bed. Instantly Fern screamed again. Katie jumped to her feet. "Okay, okay," she told Fern. "We'll walk."

Katie quickly discovered that as long as she kept moving, Fern was quiet. But the moment she stopped, the guest house filled with loud, gusty crying. She didn't think Fern's cries would attract attention. They were too far away from the Kingsleys' house or the Kramers' cabin for that. But, still, there was always a chance someone might hear. Besides, the crying was so nerve-racking, Katie couldn't stand the sound of it. She walked around the bedroom for awhile, then moved out to the living room.

The moonlight threw large patterns of silver-blue light across the floor and furniture. For awhile, Katie amused herself by walking along their outlines. After more than an hour of walking, Fern's eyes were still wide open. Tired, arms aching, Katie dared to sit on a couch.

Yowls from Fern drove her back up. "I can't take much more of this," she murmured to Fern. "Please, *please* go to sleep."

Fern quieted down and Katie walked for another hour. As she walked she became aware of a fragrance in the air. "I know that smell," Katie said aloud, trying hard to place it. Then she remembered and stood still in the moonlight, her heart racing.

The smell was of a perfume called White Lace.

It was the perfume her mother always wore.

What did this mean? Katie sniffed the air. It *was* White Lace. There was no doubt.

Fern let out a low, unhappy yowl.

Katie jiggled her as she began walking once again. "Mom?" she whispered. "Is it you?"

No answer came, but Katie continued to smell the perfume. Was her mother there?

Katie kept walking, but after a few minutes, she noticed that Fern felt lighter. Katie's arms no longer ached. It was as if some invisible hand were supporting

Fern. Looking down, she saw that Fern's eyes were closed.

"At last!" Katie sighed, settling on the couch. The lilting scent of White Lace surrounded her.

"Mom, are you here with me?" she asked. "You are, I know you are. I can feel it. I smell your perfume."

Katie ached to see her mother, to feel her warm arms around her. But sensing her presence was almost enough. "Mom, what should I do about Fern?" Katie asked desperately. She felt suddenly swamped with fatigue. She was tired of walking, but even more tired of relying on her own judgment. Since she'd found Fern, Katie hadn't stopped thinking hard about what to do. Her brain was even more exhausted than her overworked limbs. "Mom, *you* know. What should I do?"

But no answer came as Katie sat holding the baby among the neat geometric patterns of moonlight. She shook her head wearily. Of course there was no answer. She was probably just so tired she was imagining things. Resting her head against the back of the couch, Katie shut her eyes. *Just for a moment*, she told herself.

When Katie opened her eyes again, she knew instantly that something was different. Blinking to full wakefulness she looked around. The patterns of moonlight had shifted. Was that what was different?

No! It was Fern! She was no longer in Katie's arms. Katie jumped to her feet, frantically looking around.

Fern was gone!

Katie's heart raced wildly. Where was she? Had someone come in and taken her?

Nearly faint with anxiety, Katie put her hand to her head. *What do I do? What do I do?* she asked herself, fighting down panic. *I have to look for her. I'll go get Ashley.*

Dashing into the bedroom for her shoes, Katie stopped short in the doorway.

Fern was asleep on the bed with a pillow on either side of her.

"Did I do that?" Katie whispered. She didn't remember doing it. But maybe she'd been so tired that . . . no. She didn't do it.

Walking to the bedside, Katie gazed down at the quiet baby. Something in Fern's mouth glinted in the moonlight and Katie bent to look closer. "A tooth," she said softly. Fern had a new tooth in the middle of her upper gums. "So that was what all the fuss was about."

Katie yawned widely as she tossed away one pillow and climbed into bed beside Fern. "Sleep tight little Fer—" She stopped short as a gasp took her breath away.

Fern lay covered in a pink, white, and blue woven baby blanket. It was a blanket Katie had never seen before. All the same, it seemed oddly familiar.

13

"Are you *sure* you didn't bring this blanket into the guest house?" Katie whispered to Ashley the next day when she sat in the back seat of Ashley's brothers' beat-up old car with Ashley and Christina. Fern wriggled on her lap, wrapped in the lightly woven blue, white, and pink baby blanket that had mysteriously appeared the night before.

Before answering, Ashley cast an anxious glance at her twin brothers, Jason and Jeremy, in the front seat. "I'm sure," Ashley whispered. "I've never seen that blanket before. And why would I sneak in a blanket without telling you?"

"I don't know. You might have forgotten, and then I picked up the blanket without realizing . . . and then wrapped Fern in it when I was sleep walking or . . . I don't know," Katie replied. All morning she'd been struggling to find a possible explanation. There had to be one. Blankets didn't just *appear* out of nowhere.

"This is too awesome," Christina said quietly. "Someone put this blanket there, and it wasn't one of us." She chewed her lip thoughtfully. "I just had a thought. Do you think Fern's mother came and put the blanket over her?"

Katie stared at Christina, wide-eyed. That thought hadn't even occurred to her. The very idea made her hold Fern tighter. Was Fern's mother lurking around somewhere? Was she spying on her?

Of course, it was as possible as any other explanation. However that blanket had gotten there, it was strange.

Katie remembered smelling the White Lace. She'd wondered if somehow her mother—her mother's spirit, actually—had been responsible for moving the baby and putting the blanket over her. Last night Katie had had the feeling her mother was close. It was a wonderful feeling, one she wanted desperately to believe in. Yet Christina's explanation made a lot more sense.

Katie strapped Fern into the seat belt with her and kissed the warm, sweet-smelling top of her head. "Do you really think her mother is watching me, watching Fern? Why would she do that? It's creepy," she whispered.

"It's not creepy," Christina disagreed. "Maybe she's concerned about Fern. Maybe she wants to make sure she's all right."

"If she cares so much about Fern, she shouldn't have

left her in the woods," Katie hissed angrily. That act was so unforgivable that Katie had no sympathy for Fern's mother. Whatever her problem was, nothing justified such an uncaring action.

"What are you two muttering about back there?" Jason asked from the driver's seat.

"Yeah, what's the big secret?" Jeremy wanted to know. With their short carrot-red hair, green eyes, and freckles, the twins reminded Katie of older, male versions of Ashley. Lately she had no trouble telling them apart because they'd gotten new haircuts. Jason wore his hair buzzed short at the sides and curly on top, while Jeremy wore his short on the sides and top, but longish down the back of his neck.

"No secret," Ashley said quickly. "We were just talking about little Fern here."

Jason was driving them to the Pine Ridge Fire Department Halloween Picnic where they hoped to spot Fern's mother.

"She's cute," he'd said earlier. "Whose baby is she?"

The girls had looked at one another. "Uh . . . she's my cousin's," Katie had said. "I have two grown cousins in Miller's Creek. I'm baby-sitting so I have to bring her along."

Yesterday Katie didn't believe they'd find Fern's mother at the picnic and that was fine with her. But now, she wasn't as sure. Was Fern's mother trailing her, silently watching over Fern? If so, maybe she would show up at the picnic.

"Oh, no!" Jason groaned as he slowed the car.

"What?" Ashley asked.

"Motorcycle cop," Jeremy murmured grimly.

Katie turned sharply to look out the rear window. Sure enough, a helmeted officer on a motorcycle was waving them over. Jason pulled to the side of the road. "What's *his* problem? I wasn't speeding," he grumbled.

The officer came up to the window and asked for Jason's license and registration. He peered into the backseat, his eyes shielded by dark sunglasses. "That baby should be in a car seat," he said levelly.

Katie stared hard at him. Was he an angel? Was he the same officer who'd stopped them the other day when she was in the back of Spud's pickup?

No. This officer was shorter and stockier. This was the real thing.

"Sorry," Katie said. "I thought putting her in the seat belt with me would be good enough."

"No, it's not," the officer said stiffly as he wrote a ticket out and handed it to Jason. "You people are in luck. I always keep a baby seat strapped to the back of my motorcycle. Be right back."

"A baby seat strapped to his bike?" Jeremy questioned. "Is that normal?"

"Who knows?" Jason grumbled, angry about the ticket.

"I'll pay it, whatever the fine is," Katie offered. "It's my fault."

The officer came back with the car seat and helped

the girls hook it into the back seat. Christina and Ashley had to squeeze together to make room for it. Fern seemed to like the officer immediately. She reached up for him and cooed.

For a moment, the officer's stern expression cracked into a smile directed at Fern. Then it became serious again as he backed out of the car.

As the officer walked back to his motorcycle, Jason started the car. To show his annoyance, he tossed the ticket into the back seat. It fluttered into Katie's lap and she picked it up.

Her jaw dropped when she read the officer's name. Officer Winger. Jason pulled back onto the road as Katie turned back quickly to look at the officer. He stood by his bike tearing up something.

Katie drew in a deep, sharp breath. She reached across Fern and batted at Christina excitedly. "Look! Look! Look!" she whispered hoarsely. "He's tearing up the ticket. He's an angel."

Christina and Ashley whirled around to look. "I don't see him doing anything," Ashley said. "He's just getting on his bike."

"He was doing it a minute ago," Katie insisted. "And his name was Officer Winger, just like the angel yesterday, only he looked different."

Jeremy turned around in the seat wearing a bemused expression. "Katie, did I just hear you say that guy was an angel?" he asked incredulously.

Katie shot him a sheepish smile. She didn't want to

get into it because she knew Jeremy would just think she was crazy. "Well, I meant he *was* pretty cute," she said.

"Cute?" Jeremy yelped, facing front again. "Man, I'll never understand girls."

Christina mouthed the words, *Are you sure?*

Katie nodded. She'd already told them about her conversation with Ned. "Positive," she whispered.

"Wow!" Ashley and Christina said at once, their eyes as wide as saucers.

They arrived at the picnic, which was on the rolling fields behind the Pine Ridge Volunteer Fire Department. They parked and walked to the entrance.

"Hey, look at that," Jason said, pointing at a long black limousine pulling into the parking area. "Who could that be?"

They watched as the limo parked. A chauffeur in a gray suit got out and opened the back door for Molly. She spotted them immediately and waved.

"You know her?" Jeremy gasped, impressed.

"Yes, and so do you," Ashley told him tartly. "For heaven's sake, she's been trail riding at the ranch since summer, Jeremy."

"So sue me," he said, reddening. "Hey, Jason, wait up," he called to his twin, already striding ahead into the fair. The three girls stood together, rolling their eyes and giggling.

"Oooh, Jeremy has it bad," Katie snickered under her breath.

Molly joined them at the admission stand. "Do you always drive around in that?" Katie asked.

"No, but no one could drive me over so they sent the chauffeur with the limo," Molly answered matter-of-factly.

They paid the admission fee and were each given a different plastic mask with elastic straps. "It's a Halloween picnic, after all," the woman at the stand said cheerfully.

Katie put on the fox mask the woman gave her. Ashley was a rabbit and Christina a cat. "I refuse to wear this," said Molly, shoving her clown mask into the pocket of her black satin baseball jacket.

"All right now," Ashley said to them in a serious voice, pushing her mask back on top of her red hair, "keep your eyes peeled for a tall woman who looks like she's been in the woods for awhile. Mr. O'Herlihy told me she was in her early twenties, had wavy red hair, and was pretty, but scruffy. He said she had a funny accent, maybe Boston or something."

"A Boston accent. Got it," Molly said.

Katie pushed back her mask and settled Fern comfortably on her hip. The baby laughed, her dark eyes shining, as a breeze ruffled her wispy hair. "I wonder what's going to happen next," Katie said quietly, suddenly feeling very nervous.

"Well, since you mention it . . . I threw the I Ching sticks last night," Christina said from behind her mask, referring to an ancient form of Chinese fortune-telling she was trying to teach herself. "Guess what it said?"

"What?" Molly asked.

"Oh, come on, we're wasting time," Katie said impatiently. She didn't have time for this. She needed to find out if Fern's mother would be there and if she'd have to give Fern back. "I don't care what a bunch of sticks have to say."

Christina pushed up her mask and scowled at Katie. "They're *not* just a bunch of sticks. The I Ching is a centuries-old system of divination. Confucius believed in the I Ching, they think he even wrote part of it. Tell me you think Confucius was a flake. Not! And some famous Nobel Laureate physicist believed in it, too. So did the psychologist Carl Jung, and—"

"All right already! Skip the lecture," Katie interrupted. She was instantly sorry for snapping at Christina, but she was becoming more and more anxious with every passing second. "Sorry. What did the sticks say?"

"According to the book, it said, 'Heaven and earth nourish all things.'"

"Which means what?" Katie asked, shifting Fern to her other hip.

"I don't know," Christina admitted seriously. "But I thought I should pass it along."

"Thank you," Katie said, rolling her eyes. "Let's find this mother person if she's here."

The girls walked onto the field. The picnic was already crowded with adults and children, many of them wearing the masks they'd received coming in.

Most of them wandered around the vast, hilly area, others sat at picnic tables under large open-sided tents. A band stood on the wooden platform in the middle of the grounds and played soft rock. Delicious food smells from the many food stands drifted on waves of cool autumn breeze.

"Pretzels," Christina said, pointing out a wooden booth where knots of pretzel dough were being deep-fried. "Let's get some."

"Not me," Molly said, waving her hand. "Too fattening."

Christina looked at Molly sternly.

"All right, let's go," Molly said meekly, following Christina toward the pretzel stand.

Katie, Fern, and Ashley followed, too. "She's going to wind up back in the hospital if she doesn't stop thinking that way," Ashley commented.

"Christina seems to be doing a good job of staying on her case about it," Katie observed. "Maybe it's a good thing they've become friends, good for Molly, anyway."

"I suppose," Ashley agreed. "Molly's okay, really. I'm getting used to her." She looked at Fern and smiled. "Maybe she'd like to chew on a pretzel with that new tooth."

Katie shook her head. "I don't think so. She might choke."

"You're really taking good care of her, Katie," Ashley said warmly. "You'll be a good mother someday."

Katie nodded, a sad smile forming on her lips. Kind as

Ashley's complimentary words were, they reminded her that this wasn't *someday*. This was now. If her aunt and uncle didn't take Fern—and down deep Katie didn't think they would—she'd have to give Fern away to someone. It was as if she could already feel her heart starting to break.

Ashley suddenly grabbed her arm. "Over there! Look!"

Katie gazed in the direction Ashley was pointing.

Standing by a hot dog stand was a tall, attractive woman with messy red hair, a scruffy khaki army jacket over dirty jeans, and a khaki backpack slung over her shoulders.

"That could be her," Ashley said excitedly. "Everything fits."

Katie bit her lip as a hard knot formed in her stomach.

14

"Christina, Molly," Ashley called. The two girls turned toward her. "I think I see her."

Christina and Molly hurried to join Katie and Ashley.

Katie hugged Fern to her side, barely breathing.

"That woman over there," Ashley said, pointing. "Let's go see if that's Fern's mother."

"It could be," Christina agreed.

"Come on," Molly said, heading off in the woman's direction. The rest followed.

The woman had turned her back as she moved away from the hot dog stand to eat. She couldn't see them approaching.

Katie lagged several paces behind the others. "It's probably not her," she whispered to Fern. "What are the chances?" Fern smiled up at her and gurgled, showing off her new tooth. Would Fern know her mother? Katie wondered. Would she reach out happily when she saw this woman?

If Fern *did* reach for her, what would the woman do? Would she run away? Would that break Fern's heart? Would it cause a deep, deep sadness that she'd carry with her for the rest of her life?

Katie's heartbeat quickened as they neared the woman. What was going to happen? Maybe she wouldn't be Fern's mother. "Don't let it be her," she prayed fervently.

When they were just a few feet away from the woman, another woman with a small blonde child walked up to her. "Where did you get the hot dog?" the other woman asked.

The red-haired woman pointed to the hot dog stand. "Over there," pronouncing the words as *Ova thah.*

Christina, Ashley, and Molly looked at one another with excited expressions. The woman spoke with a definite accent, a Boston kind of accent. This was their woman, for sure.

"It's her," Ashley said to Katie.

Katie felt as if her heart had turned into a hummingbird with wildly beating wings. Her arms began to tremble. Fern caught her agitation and screwed up her face, preparing to howl.

No! everything inside Katie screamed. She wasn't giving up Fern!

Clutching the baby to her, she turned and ran.

"Katie!" She heard Ashley calling her, but Katie didn't

look back. She had to keep going. She had to get away from this woman who might take Fern away from her, this woman who had left Fern all alone in the woods. The woman couldn't possibly be a good mother, she couldn't really care about Fern. Fern deserved someone who could love her, really love her and take good care of her.

Katie ran through the crowd as Fern cried, red-faced in her arms. She didn't stop until she could no longer see her friends or the woman. Only then did Katie stop to catch her breath.

Panting, she tried to calm Fern by patting her back and rocking her. Slowly Fern's cries faded to a soft, sniffling whimper.

There were people on every side of her, yet Katie felt completely alone. It was as if she were in a bubble with Fern. No one could see them, and she couldn't communicate with anyone on the outside. A white-haired woman in a wheelchair came up alongside Katie. "Are you all right?" she asked. The bubble feeling shattered.

"Oh . . . uh . . . yeah. Just calming down my little sister."

"Babies really pick up on what you're feeling," the elderly woman commented, studying Katie searchingly with her steely blue eyes. "If you're upset, they get upset."

"I'm not upset," Katie lied breathlessly. "I think she's just getting another tooth."

The woman nodded. "Might I ask you a favor?"

"Sure."

"Could you push me over there to the sausage and peppers stand? See how rocky it is there? I don't think I could make it on my own."

Katie looked at the woman apologetically. "I would but I've got the baby. I'll go ask someone else who might be able—"

"I'll hold the baby on my lap," the woman said calmly but firmly, reaching out her wrinkled arms.

"I guess that would be all right," Katie agreed, handing Fern over to her.

"Hello, little darling," the white-haired woman cooed to Fern as Katie got behind the wheelchair and began to push.

Gazing over the woman's shoulder, Fern looked up at Katie with large, questioning eyes. Inwardly, Katie was pleased that Fern didn't feel comfortable with everyone. She was happy that Fern obviously wanted to come back into her arms.

"She wants you," the woman commented. "She won't take her eyes off you."

"Yeah, we're real close," Katie replied as she leaned her weight into the chair.

The old woman had been right about the rocks. Pushing the wheelchair over them was rough going. Katie was almost to the long table in front of a flat open grill full of sausages and fried peppers sizzling in baking pans when the woman tending the grill let out a horrified scream.

Katie turned and looked up sharply at the screaming woman. Foot-high flames shot up from the grill while a lower line of fire spread rapidly along it.

"The fire extinguisher! Where is it?" the woman shrieked frantically. "Where is it?"

With a darting glance, Katie spotted the red cylinder lying on its side in front of the table. Letting go of the wheelchair, she dove for it. "Here it is!" she cried, lifting the fire extinguisher shoulder high. A man came and took it from her hands. In seconds he had sprayed the white foam over the grill, soaking the pans of sausages and peppers.

"Thank you," the grill woman told Katie. "Thank goodness you saw it lying there. It must have rolled under the table."

"No problem," Katie said with a smile. She turned back to the woman in the wheelchair.

Where was she?

Katie looked around in all directions. How could she have disappeared so quickly? She was in a wheelchair!

She had Fern!

At that moment, Ashley, Christina, and Molly burst through the crowd of people that had gathered to see the fire. "There you are!" Ashley cried when she saw Katie.

"Where's Fern?" Christina asked at the same time.

"A woman took her," Katie cried. "An old woman in a wheelchair. I have to find her."

"What happened?" Molly asked.

Tears sprang to Katie's eyes, but she couldn't give in to them. "I'll explain later. We have to find her. Please, help me look."

"A woman in a wheelchair can't have gone far," Ashley said as she looked in every direction. "We'll find her."

"We *have* to find her," Katie said, her voice a sob. "Spread out."

"We have to tell an adult," Molly said.

Katie looked at her, speechless. Once they told adults about Fern, they'd take her away. Still, they had no choice now.

"All right," Katie agreed. Fern's safety was more important than anything else. "Tell someone in charge. Then everyone will be looking for her."

"Come on," Christina said to Molly. "We'll go tell that woman over there." The two girls ran toward a woman in full firefighter's dress standing by a red hook and ladder truck.

"Don't worry. We'll find her," Ashley said once again as she hurried off to look for Fern.

Katie ran through the crowd, frantically looking at everyone and everything she passed. "Have you seen a woman in a wheelchair with a baby?" she asked strangers. When they shook their heads, she moved on to the next stranger. "Seen an old woman in a wheelchair with a baby?"

Where could she have gone? And why? What did the old woman want with Fern? Was she a kidnapper? Was the wheelchair just a ploy to put people off guard?

That had to be it! She couldn't have moved so quickly if she was still in that wheelchair.

Katie was furious with herself. How could she have been so stupid? The woman must have spotted her immediately. An upset girl with a crying baby—a perfect target.

What would she do with Fern? Would she keep her? Sell her to someone? Katie felt her heart twinge at the thought.

As Katie moved, sharp-eyed, through the crowd, she spotted the tall red-haired woman. The one who might be Fern's mother. Should she tell her what had happened?

Yes, Katie decided. If she *was* Fern's mother, she should know.

But, as Katie moved toward the woman, she moved further away. She was hurrying somewhere, heading toward the parking lot. Katie noticed she was carrying a large picnic basket. From the way she leaned to one side, it seemed to be quite heavy. Katie guessed maybe she'd packed up a lot of the free food. "Wait," she called. "Wait up."

The woman looked over her shoulder at Katie. For a moment their eyes locked. Then the woman began to run.

15

Katie ran after the woman, but she moved fast. Quickly she managed to put a lot of distance between Katie and herself.

As Katie chased after her, weaving and darting through the crowd, she wondered why the woman was running from her. What did she have to hide? Were the police after her or something like that?

Katie burst free of the crowd when she reached the parking lot. Panting, she scanned the area, searching for the woman. Katie knew she had to find her before she got into her car. If she drove away, Katie would never find her. Katie began running among the parked cars, hoping to find the woman as she got into one of them.

There! Katie spotted her over by the bike rack, strapping the basket to the back of a bike.

The next thing Katie saw made her freeze. The

woman opened the basket and bent over it.

A small baby arm shot out.

"Fern!" Katie shouted as she ran toward the woman. Fern was in the basket. It had to be! That woman hadn't had a baby with her when they first saw her. But how had she gotten hold of Fern?

The woman looked up and spotted Katie running toward her. Her eyes grew wide with alarm. She shut the basket, hopped on her bike, and raced off.

Katie stood for a moment, feeling as if she were in a dream. The woman was taking Fern away.

"No way," Katie said firmly, snapping out of her dream state.

Without thinking, she grabbed an unchained bike and jumped on. She was just borrowing it, she'd bring it back, Katie told herself, hopefully before its owner even knew it was gone. But right now she was desperate.

Pedaling madly, she rode past the fire department up to the main road. Peering down the two-lane stretch of asphalt, she spied the woman on the bike.

Katie pushed down hard on the pedals. This woman wasn't going to ride off with Fern just like that. Katie just couldn't live with herself if she let Fern go without making sure she was safe. Maybe this woman was a criminal. That had to be it. Otherwise why didn't she just come up to Katie and ask her to give her daughter back?

This crazy woman was riding with Fern in a picnic basket. What if the basket broke or fell off the bike? It certainly wasn't safe.

Cars went by, oblivious of Katie's problem. Where was Officer Winger now that she needed him?

Katie pumped the pedals as fast as she could, but the woman ahead of her soon disappeared around a bend in the road.

No, Katie thought. *I can't lose sight of her. I can't let her get away from me.*

Despite not being able to see the woman, Katie didn't slacken her pace. There was still a chance she could catch up. The woman might stop or fall or slow down. As long as there was any possibility of closing in on her, Katie was determined to keep going.

Skidding around the curve, Katie struggled to keep her balance and continued on, head bent, leg muscles burning but relentless. About a half-mile later, she jammed on the brakes, causing her bike to slide unnervingly into the fallen leaves alongside the road before she was able to stop.

At the edge of the woods, the woman's bike leaned against a pine at an odd angle, as if she'd thrown it down in a hurry. The lid of the picnic basket hung open, and the basket was clearly empty.

She's hiding in the woods, Katie realized, leaping off her borrowed bike and letting it bang into the abandoned one.

Breathing hard, Katie walked into the woods, following a natural break in the trees. But which way? Which way? she wondered. The woods seemed completely empty, but the woman had to have come in this way with Fern. Otherwise Katie would have seen her going down the road.

Suddenly, Katie froze and cocked her head, listening intently. Off in the distance, she heard the sharp crack of a branch breaking.

Katie began running swiftly but lightly toward the sound, hoping it wasn't just some animal in the woods, praying the crack was made by the woman who was carrying Fern away.

As Katie dashed through the trees, she realized she was probably in the Pine Manor woods. She'd just entered from a different direction than usual. Sure, it *had* to be the same woods. The road she'd just been on led to the Pine Manor Ranch. This was just further into the woods than they usually traveled when they entered from the ranch side.

Then, all at once, she heard the high-pitched wail of a baby crying.

Good girl, Fern! Katie cheered silently. *Way to go! Keep crying and I'll find you.*

Fern continued to scream as Katie moved quickly and steadily toward the sound. Katie soon realized she was following the course of a creek. Not the same one she'd followed the other day. This one was different, narrower and more shallow.

The woman was following the creek, Katie guessed. *Great!* Now even if Fern stopped crying, Katie would still be able to catch up with her.

Fern's cries continued, though, echoing through the

woods. Katie ran even faster, encouraged now that it seemed possible to find Fern. She followed the creek and soon became aware of another sound. It was rushing water, the sound of a waterfall.

The swirling pool!

The woman must be taking Fern back to the abandoned campsite where Katie had first found her!

Fern's cries died down, but it no longer mattered. Katie had figured out where she could find her. All she had to do was continue following the creek. It would lead her to the pool. From there she could find the campsite.

But she'd have to hurry. If the woman didn't stay at the campsite, Katie might lose her altogether. Katie couldn't imagine living the rest of her life not knowing what became of Fern.

Pressing on, Katie came into the grove of white birches with their shimmering pale yellow leaves. She was heartened at this sign she was moving in the right direction.

A cold shiver ran through her. The air was colder here. Maybe because she was deeper in the forest or because she was approaching the waterfalls, she wasn't sure.

Finally Katie came to a place where the creek widened. It picked up force from a spring that gushed from the base of a boulder near the water's edge.

"I'm coming, Fern," Katie whispered, hoping the sheer strength of her love could send her message to Fern. "I'm almost there. Don't worry."

As Katie tracked the stream's path she wondered how Fern was feeling. Was she happy to be back with her mother? *Was* this woman even her mother?

Was Fern scared? Did she wonder what had happened to Katie? Was she angry at Katie for losing her like this? Katie couldn't stand the thought that Fern might think she'd abandoned her.

Katie reached a spot where the creek picked up speed and poured over a rock ledge. Looking down, she saw a waterfall gushing down into the swirling pool. The force of the falling water sent up clouds of misty spray.

Across the pool was the first waterfall. Around it all stood the majestic ring of towering pines. Once again, Katie was overwhelmed by the feeling that this was a somehow magical spot.

Birds swooped around the pool, winging their way from tree to tree, just as they had the day she'd first seen it. Was it the water that attracted them? she wondered. Or was it the almost magical energy of the place?

Katie struggled to orient herself. Which way was the campsite from here? She wasn't exactly sure, but she knew it wasn't far. The other day she'd been in the swirling pool when she heard Fern's cries. It might help to go down to the pool and try to figure out her direction from there.

Moving fast and spreading her arms wide for balance, she went down the rocky side of the waterfall. The cold water sprayed her as she went. The wet rocks were slippery. Katie slipped and fell on her bottom. "Ow!" She decided to stay seated and slide her way down.

As she slid, a sound rose up above the steady roar of the waterfall. It was familiar, but Katie couldn't place it. Was it a bird calling?

Katie grabbed hold of the rock and stopped moving. She'd identified the sound.

It was the sound of baby gurgling happily, laughing.

Fern!

But where was she?

Katie frantically looked all around. Where could she possibly be?

Fern laughed again.

Katie stopped moving and drew in a careful breath. With a slow, intent gaze she took in everything around her.

All at once she gasped, almost unable to believe her eyes.

Fern was sitting on a glistening, water-sprayed shelf of rock jutting out from the middle of the waterfall next to her. She hadn't been able to see her when she'd looked down from above because of the cloud of heavy mist created by the spraying water.

Fern sat on the same rock ledge on which the crow had perched the other day when it dropped her locket into the pool below.

On either side of Fern, water cascaded into the pool like matching silvery-white drapes. The baby squealed in delight, waving her arms as the water sprayed her with a fine tickling mist. Her pink stretchy suit was soaked and her fine, soft hair had curled in the mist, but Fern seemed completely happy.

How had she gotten up there? That horrible woman must have put her there, but how?

The ledge was exactly in the middle of the waterfall. It seemed too high to reach from below, and too low to reach from above. Katie didn't think it could be reached from the sides, either.

Studying the situation, Katie saw that a rotted, fallen tree lay on its side over the bend at the top of the waterfall. Water rushed over its spindly branches. The tree might offer some access to the rock ledge below it, but surely it was too fragile for a person to climb out on.

"Fern," Katie whispered, creeping slowly forward. She didn't want to startle her by speaking loudly. She didn't want her to move at all.

Fern saw her and smiled brightly in greeting. Eagerly, she stretched out her pudgy arms as if reaching for Katie.

Unbalanced by her outstretched arms, Fern tumbled forward, precariously closer to the edge of the rock ledge. She looked up at Katie and smiled.

"Don't move, Fern," Katie said evenly, praying the baby might somehow understand her. She held her hands up. "Stay there. Don't move."

Fern tried to sit up, but her small hands slipped

back on the wet rock. Again, she giggled as if it were all a game.

Katie held her breath as she considered a terrifying possibility Fern was blissfully unaware of. At any moment Fern could slip from the ledge and plummet into the swirling water below.

And Katie hadn't the slightest idea of how to reach her.

16

"Think, Katie, think," Katie urged herself in a desperate whisper. With darting glances, she checked in all directions, looking for the tall, red-haired woman. Where had she gone?

She seemed to have somehow disappeared. Katie stopped looking. She couldn't spend any more time searching. She had to reach Fern before she fell.

Fern was now frighteningly close to the edge, her one leg dangling playfully in the air. Her laugh floated up over the roar of the waterfall.

It might be possible to climb back up the rocky side of the waterfall and then leap over to the rock ledge.

Possible, but dangerous.

It would be a long jump and the ledge was slippery. There was also the possibility that she might knock Fern off when she landed. *That would be terrible*, Katie thought, gasping at the idea.

Katie squared her shoulders with grim determination. She would just have to be careful, she resolved.

With her eyes constantly on Fern, Katie climbed up the side of the waterfall until she was even with the ledge.

From her glistening, misty perch, Fern sat, happily watching Katie.

Crouching, Katie steadied herself, preparing to jump.

"Now!" she shouted wildly. With every muscle straining, Katie sprang from her crouching position. In seconds she was flying through air, forcing herself to keep her eyes open. She had to be able to see so she could grab the rock without unsettling Fern.

Time seemed to move in slow motion. Katie saw Fern come nearer and nearer. The wet rock shone. She was almost there.

Yes! she cheered silently as the rock slammed into her midriff. She'd made it!

Reaching out, Katie clawed at the smooth, wet surface of the rock ledge. But the surface was too slippery. Her fingers slipped, scrabbling for something to grab.

From the corner of her eye, she saw Fern looking at her with knit, perplexed brows.

The next thing Katie knew, she was sliding off the rock. With a cry of panic, she tumbled backward, spread-eagled, into the swirling pool below.

Inches from the water, Katie instinctively took a huge

gulp of air and clamped her lips shut before she plunged under the icy surface.

The freezing water swept around her with unexpected force. Katie struggled to raise her head above the surface, but the current kept beating her back as it held her in the grip of its surging vortex.

She felt like a piece clothing in some super-strong washing machine as it swirled through the spin cycle. Slowly, though, Katie realized she was being pulled deeper and deeper.

A sound filled her head as she flailed her arms, struggling helplessly. It was like singing—an incredible chorus of high, sweet voices singing in a language she couldn't understand.

Katie wondered if she were drowning.

Then—suddenly—it was as if watery hands lifted her up, higher and higher, until her head broke the surface of the water. Her mouth shot open to feed her bursting lungs.

Gasping, Katie checked the rock ledge. Fern was still there. *Thank goodness.*

A small boulder nearby gave Katie something to grab and pull herself out of the water. She looked back at the stream. The other day when she'd waded in after her locket she'd had no idea the pool was so deep or its current so strong. If she hadn't heard Fern crying, Katie might have walked right into it. Who knew if she would have been as lucky then as she had been today? Maybe hearing Fern's cries had saved her life.

Katie wondered what had saved her life today. Probably another current surging upward. That was the logical explanation. Yet it had definitely felt like someone was pushing her.

And what about the song she heard? Probably just the ringing of her ears or the water surging around her.

Katie couldn't worry about it for long. She still had to get to Fern.

Looking up, she drew in a sharp breath of surprise and alarm.

On the fallen tree lying over the waterfall was an red fox. With agile steps, it picked its way over the tree's brittle branches, its small, black eyes trained directly on Fern.

"Go away!" Katie shouted. When she reached the water's edge, she grabbed a heavy rock and hurled it at the fox. The rock glanced off the tree, bouncing up next to the fox. The fox sprang back, its bushy, white-tipped tail standing up in surprise. But, after a moment, it continued on its way.

Katie threw another rock, which flew high over the tree without the fox even noticing. The next rock she threw came dangerously close to Fern before it whizzed past the fox's ears. Again, it jumped back, but continued on after a short while.

Did the fox think Fern was dinner? She was certainly helpless prey.

The fox stopped at the end of the tree and leaned out over the empty space, so sure of its balance that it was unafraid of the long drop. The animal studied Fern just below, and Katie didn't like the look on its face. It was a sharp, hungry look, she thought.

"Go away!" she screamed again, but the fox didn't even acknowledge her.

Katie had come out of the water on the bank opposite the side she'd climbed down. What would it take to climb to that tree? This side of the waterfall was thick with thorny-looking bushes, but she couldn't worry about thorns now. She had to get to Fern. Nothing else mattered.

Katie pushed her way into the thicket, grimacing as the tiny thorns spiked her hands and wrists. She held her arms over her head and pressed on. Raising her arms caused her heavy, dripping shirt and jacket to rise up, exposing her rib cage. "Ahhh," she moaned as the thorns bit into her like sharp teeth.

As she pushed through the bushes, she kept her eyes on Fern and the fox. Fern giggled and reached up to the fox, treating it like a pet or a plaything.

Thorns tore at Katie's soaked clothes. Katie's sweatshirt started to tear along one side. The thorns clung to the fleecy inside of the material. "Ow! Ow!" Katie cringed as she tried to pick them off. The more she worked at freeing herself, it seemed the more deeply ensnarled in the thorny branches she became.

With light-footed grace, the fox leapt from the end of the tree and dropped easily down onto the ledge next to Fern.

Katie clawed at the bushes, trying to ignore the pain. She had to get there! How had she gotten so hopelessly tangled in these horrible thorns? Now she was stuck here and the fox was next to Fern. If it attacked her, there wouldn't be a thing Katie could do about it.

17

Katie's attention was diverted from the fox by a new movement on the overhanging tree. A fat raccoon waddled out. Despite its clumsy appearance, it moved confidently over the branches.

Recalling Uncle Jeff's warnings about raccoons, Katie grew even more worried. They had razor-sharp claws and could be nasty if cornered. Besides, this raccoon was out in the daytime. Usually you only saw them at night. A daytime raccoon sometimes meant the animal had rabies.

Remembering the fox, Katie looked back and, to her complete surprise, saw that it had curled up into a ball and fallen asleep beside Fern. What was more, Fern was lying on his fur, sleeping peacefully while the water cascaded down on either side of her.

How totally strange, Katie thought.

The raccoon made it to the end of the tree and looked down. At the same time, the fox lifted its head and sniffed the air. It took only seconds for it to locate the source of the smell. Looking up, the fox spied the raccoon looking down.

Instantly, the fox scrambled up on its slender legs and Fern slid off. Blinking in confusion, she rubbed her eyes with her pudgy fists, then propped herself on her side.

Baring its small, sharp white teeth, the fox emitted a low growl. Instantly, the raccoon backed away. The fox barked at it, a high, shrill yip. That sent the raccoon scrambling over the tree and back into the forest.

Stuck in the brambles, Katie watched in awed disbelief. This fox seemed to be protecting Fern. She felt an intense surge of gratitude toward the animal. If she couldn't be there to protect Fern, at least the fox was helping.

Katie was struck with a comparison. If her parents were spirits now, did they look over her from afar? And if they did, were they frustrated that they couldn't reach her, couldn't help her more directly the way they used to? Did they long to get to her as she now longed to reach Fern? Did they feel the same overwhelming gratitude toward Aunt Rainie and Uncle Jeff as she now felt toward the fox?

She suspected that the answer was yes.

As Katie thought these things, she slowly became aware of a fragrance in the air. It invaded her senses subtly at first, so that she was only vaguely aware of it.

But, little by little, its strength grew until it captured her full attention.

It wasn't pine. Could it be the scent of some nearby autumn flower? She didn't see any.

It was White Lace!

But how? Why?

Movement at her hip made her look. Wide-eyed, she watched as the thorny hold on her shirt was released as if by an invisible hand. As she moved forward the thorny bushes parted easily for her.

"Mom?" she whispered. "Mom?"

A breeze ruffled her wet hair—a breeze that felt so very much like the gentle caress of a loving hand sweeping across her hair.

Katie reached out with both hands, yearning to feel her mother. "I know you're near," she said, for the first time ever, feeling the certainty deep in her heart. "Is Dad with you? Daddy, are you here?"

Another warm breeze swept past like fingers brushing her cheek. Katie pressed her hand to her cheek, wanting to capture the feeling.

With a darting glance, she checked Fern on the ledge. She was surprised to see that a second fox had joined the first one. It must have come out onto the tree while she wasn't looking.

The baby's eyes shone while the second fox efficiently, yet tenderly, licked her round cheek, as if it were cleaning its own cubs.

Katie blinked back tears. What was going on? This

was all so confusing. She thought of Aunt Rainie and Uncle Jeff. They *did* try to take care of her as if she was one of their own. She was suddenly sure they didn't treat her any differently than they'd treated their own grown daughters. Uncle Jeff probably drove them crazy with his complaining about the bills, too, Katie realized. She'd been taking it personally, but she now understood that it wasn't personal. It was just how he was. Maybe even Mel was simply acting toward her the way he'd acted toward his own sisters. It was possible, even probable.

Katie checked the ledge again.

Her jaw dropped and her hands flew to cover her gaping mouth.

The rock was now ablaze with a shimmering white light that was nearly blinding. At the center of the light hovered two magnificent, celestial angels dressed in robes of silver and gold. Impossibly, huge white wings fanned out behind them.

And they held Fern lifted up between them.

Katie squinted hard, straining to see into the light. The angels' faces—she knew them! The one with flowing blonde curls was Edwina. Katie recognized her soft, beautiful face. The silky black hair of the other angel belonged to Norma. So did the straight, dignified features. Their identical violet-blue eyes blazed with warmth and love.

The rapturous spell was broken by the sound of footsteps crashing through the woods at the far side of the waterfall. "I think I see her," Katie heard someone cry. It was Ashley. In the next moment, her friends burst into view above the waterfall.

They stopped short, clutching one another in awe. From the amazement on their faces, Katie knew they, too, could see the unbelievable vision on the ledge.

As the girls stared, transfixed with amazement, Edwina and Norma effortlessly lifted Fern into the air. The baby seemed to float on the tips of their delicate, graceful fingers.

Katie gasped.

Fern had wings!

Wings! Feathery and small, just perfect for a delicate, laughing, baby angel.

"Fern," Katie breathed, reaching up toward the baby she loved so much. Fern looked at her with an expression filled with warm affection.

She smiled at Katie, her dark eyes now shining a soft violet-blue. Then she rose up into the air. Katie didn't take her eyes off Fern until she was up near the trees.

Like a shimmering bubble that suddenly pops, Fern disappeared.

Katie looked back at the ledge. Norma and Edwina were gone, too.

"Katie!" Christina called as she came quickly down the rocky side of the waterfall, half running, half sliding, with Molly and Ashley hurrying behind. "Katie, are you all right?"

Katie opened her mouth to answer, but discovered

she was too stunned and filled with emotion to say anything. Her mind reeled, trying to make sense of everything that had happened.

Her friends reached the other side of the swirling pool, but couldn't find a way across. Katie glanced at the water and saw that the whirlpool—with its madly spinning vortex—had disappeared. The water moved, but without the force it had possessed before.

Slowly, still dazed, she waded into it. As she did, she became aware, once again, of the scent of White Lace in the air. She stopped, ankle deep in cold water, closed her eyes, and inhaled deeply.

The scent lingered a moment, then faded slowly away.

"Katie, are you sick? Are you okay?" Ashley called urgently.

"I'm okay," Katie said, opening her eyes. She slogged through the pool in her heavy, saturated clothing.

So Fern had been an angel. Fern was an angel. The thought played itself over and over in her head. Katie couldn't get it to make sense. She'd found a baby angel lost in the woods.

But had Fern ever been *really* lost?

Had she come to Katie for a reason? What was the reason?

When Katie was halfway across, Ashley and Christina rushed into the water and grabbed hold of her, supporting her. "Fern was an angel," she told them, still dreamy with amazement.

"We know," Ashley said seriously.

"We saw," Christina added.

From the shore, Molly nodded. "You'd better get her out of that water," she said. "She's shivering."

Molly's words made Katie realize she *was* trembling with cold. Leaning heavily on her friends, the girls walked toward the water's edge together.

Just as Katie was about to step onto the rocky bank, she noticed something silver sparkling in the crystal clear water beneath her feet.

18

"My locket!" Katie gasped as she bent to pick up the silver object at her feet. It was icy to the touch, as though it had been in a freezer.

"What locket?" Christina asked. "You didn't have that on at the picnic. I would have remembered seeing it."

"I didn't," Katie replied, snapping open the cold, wet locket. Miraculously, the pictures inside weren't completely ruined, just rippled slightly with damp. With shining, happy eyes, her parents' faces smiled up at Katie and the warm breeze swept past her cheeks.

"Oh, I remember now!" Christina said. "That's the locket the crow stole from you the other day. Oh, my gosh, the crow must have been . . . oh, my gosh. Maybe it led you here just so you'd find Fern."

Katie gazed down at her parents faces for a long moment, losing herself in the memory of her mother's perfume, of feeling the warm breeze like a loving caress against her cheek.

"Katie," Ashley said softly, her voice floating to Katie on a dreamy cloud. "Katie."

When Katie looked up at her, Ashley's face was filled with gentle concern. "You should get out of the water."

Only then did Katie realize she was still standing in the pool. Ashley reached out and took her arm as Katie stepped onto the bank.

"Here," Christina said, struggling out of her purple woolen jacket. "Put this on. You're shivering."

"I'm okay," Katie told her, but Christina draped the jacket across her shoulders anyway.

"You'd better sit," Molly said quietly.

Katie found a flat rock and sat, still gazing at her locket. After awhile she realized that her friends were unnaturally quiet and she looked up. The three girls stood, each of them lost in her own thoughts, staring blankly out at the tranquil landscape as if dazed.

Ashley was the first to notice her. "Are you all right?"

Katie nodded. "I'm not sure why all this happened. Why should I find a baby angel in the woods? Do you think it meant something, that it was for a reason?"

Christina sat down cross-legged on the ground. "It always means something."

Katie knew she was right. The angels weren't frivolous with their appearance. It was always for a reason.

Then, with a sudden jolt of understanding, Katie knew. She'd found Fern and learned to love her. It was as if the door to her heart, which had been shut so tightly when her parents died, had been pried open by her love for Fern. Sure, she'd gotten over the immediate, shocked grief. She'd even thought she was fine. She hadn't been fine, though.

She'd been afraid to love anyone ever again.

And if she couldn't—wouldn't—love anyone, she could never believe anyone would love her. For the rest of her life, Katie would have lived in a world without love. That feeling, that miserable certainty, had been a great, deep sadness coursing beneath the surface of her being like a poisoned underground stream.

Fern had touched that stream with her beauty and sweetness. And the magic of Katie's love for the baby had touched the stream and transformed it into something crystal, bracing and clear.

Katie now knew that despite all her pain, she *could* love again. People would love her, too. Seeing with the eyes of love made her realize how Aunt Rainie loved her already, and how Uncle Jeff tried in his own clumsy way to love her.

She studied the pictures in her locket. Her parents, too, had loved her deeply. That love hadn't died. It was in her. Katie was now confident that if her parents could reach her or help her in any way, they would. They already had.

There was so much more to think about. Had Fern's mother been an angel, too? Was she Edwina? Was the woman in the wheelchair Norma?

"Katie, your face," Ashley said, sounding surprised.

Katie touched her cheeks self-consciously. "What about it?"

"I don't know. It's your expression. You look so . . . so . . . happy, I guess," Ashley said.

"I think I am happy," Katie said. "I feel really happy inside." She leaned back and looked at the trees and smelled the pine-scented air. A feeling of pure joy bubbled up from somewhere deep inside her and escaped in a burst of laughter. "Something's changed," Katie said, astounded by this rush of ebullient happiness. "The trees even look greener to me. The water looks brighter."

"You've been touched by angels," Molly said.

"Yes," Katie said, getting to her feet. "I have."

"We all have," Christina added. "Whenever I see them I feel . . . I feel . . . I can't describe it."

"Blessed?" Molly offered.

"Hmmm . . . blessed?" Christina tested the sound of the word. "Maybe that's it. I'm not sure. I feel touched. Moved. Yes! For me, moved is the word. Like something inside me has moved, gotten better somehow. Healthier. Stronger."

"Blessed. Moved. What does it matter if you call it by one word or the other?" Ashley said. "I think it's the same thing. We're all changed every time we come near the angels."

Christina looked at the locket in Katie's hand. "And you found your locket again. How strange."

Katie wrapped her fingers around the locket and put it in her jacket pocket. "How did you find me?" she asked.

"I saw you running after the woman with the picnic basket," Molly said. "I figured she must have Fern or you wouldn't be chasing her."

"Darrin Tyson was leaving the picnic with his older sister, so we piled into the car with them and came looking for you to see if we could help," Ashley continued. "Then we spotted the bikes just off the road. We asked his sister to pull over and we jumped out."

"Uh-oh," said Katie. "That means everyone back at the picnic is still looking for Fern."

Ashley's pale complexion grew paler. "That's right. What will we tell them?"

"We'll just say it was a mistake," Molly suggested. "We'll say Katie was baby-sitting her cousin's little girl and she didn't realize that her cousin had come to pick up the baby."

"That will work," Katie agreed.

"They're going to be mad," Christina worried.

"Well, there's nothing we can do about it," Molly said, unconcerned. "They'll get over it."

The girls climbed up the rocky side of the waterfall. Before re-entering the woods, Katie drank in the sight of the pool, the waterfalls, and the pines so busy with the singing birds. She looked at the shimmering birches. Would she ever be able to find this spot again? she wondered. Or was it part of the mysterious, angelic experience she'd just had? Would it disappear just as Fern, Norma, and Edwina had disappeared?

"Bye, Fern," Katie whispered as a lump formed in her throat. "I won't forget you."

"Come on, Katie," called Ashley, who, along with Christina and Molly, had gone further into the woods.

With a last, lingering glance, Katie hurried to join them. They walked through the woods and came out onto the road at a different spot than where they'd entered. "We're going to have to walk back," Ashley said with a miserable sigh.

"No, we won't," Molly disagreed confidently. She reached into the pocket of her satin baseball jacket and pulled out a hand-sized cellular phone. She punched in a number and then spoke to someone on the other end. "Terence, I'll be walking along Route 100 toward the picnic. Could you come and pick up my friends and me? Thank you." She turned to the others. "The limo is on its way."

Christina, Katie, and Ashley exchanged glances and then started laughing.

"What?" Molly asked, perplexed by their amusement. "What's so funny."

"We're just not used to being picked up by limos," Katie laughed.

Molly went pink with embarrassment. "Well," she said with shrug. "What's a limo? It's just a big car."

"Do you always carry a cellular phone?" Ashley asked her.

"It was a birthday present," Molly answered. "It comes in very handy."

"I bet," Katie laughed.

"It probably does," Christina said. "Hey, why don't we just call them at the picnic and tell them we found Fern?"

It sounded like a good idea to Katie. That way if anyone was angry, she wouldn't have to deal with it face to face. But she knew that was the coward's way out. "Oh, we'll just go tell them. If they're mad, they're mad," she said.

"You're right," Christina groaned. "But I wish you weren't."

They began walking along the road. When they came to the spot where Katie had left the bikes, the one with the picnic basket was gone. Only Katie's borrowed bike remained. She was happy to see that despite the rough treatment she'd given it, there were no dents or scratches on the bike. In fact, it looked better than she remembered. Maybe she simply hadn't looked at it very carefully the first time.

Terence drove up with the limo and put the bike in the trunk. Together, the girls climbed into the roomy back seat. It seemed to Katie that they glided, rather than drove back to the picnic.

"I'll do this," Katie said bravely when they arrived at the picnic grounds. She got out of the limo and found a woman in a red polo shirt with the Pine Ridge fire-fighter's insignia on it. She explained that her cousin had taken Fern. "I just didn't know she had her," she said.

The woman frowned at Katie, then she nodded. "Better to be safe than sorry," she said with a resigned sigh. "You did the right thing. I'll make an announcement over the public address system."

"Thank you," Katie said, relieved that the woman had stayed calm.

As Katie walked back to the limo, she saw two girls by the bike rack wearing distressed expressions. They looked enough alike that Katie guessed they were sisters. The shorter one looked close to tears. "I told you to get a lock," the taller one said.

"I can't believe it's gone!" the shorter girl cried, flapping her arms helplessly.

Katie swallowed hard. How was she going to explain this one? She'd just have to do it.

"Wait!" she called, approaching the girls. "I have your bike. I took it before and—"

"You took my bike?" the girl cried angrily. "Where is it? Give it back!"

"I will, I will," Katie assured her. "It's in the trunk of that limo over there."

The shorter girl put her hands on her slim hips and eyed Katie skeptically. The older girl folded her arms and glared.

Katie heard a limo door open and saw Molly jump out and run to the trunk. She lifted out the bike and wheeled it toward Katie and the girls. "See, there it is," Katie said.

As Molly got closer with the bike, the shorter girl ran to it. "Hey, that's not my bike!" she cried, whirling around toward Katie accusingly. "What are you trying to pull?"

"Sorry," Katie said. "I took a bike. I thought it was yours."

The girl studied the bike. "Those *do* look like the streamers on my bike."

"That's the same license plate you had on the back," her older sister noted. "Check under the seat. Remember? You wrote your name under the seat."

Molly held the bike while the girl looked. "It *is* my bike!" she cried. "But it looks brand new or something. What did you do to it?"

Katie lifted her arms in a gesture of bewilderment. "I didn't do anything."

"Well, thanks. Thanks for making it new," the girl said.

"Sure. No problem," Katie told her as she and Molly exchanged knowing glances.

Molly and Katie climbed back into the limo just as Ashley spied Jason and Jeremy heading back to the car. "I'll drop you off at home," Molly offered. "Well, Terence will, I mean."

Ashley ran to tell her brothers they didn't need a ride, then got back into the limo. "That was sweet," she reported. "They were looking for us because they figured we must be so completely mortified we'd want to leave."

"That *was* thoughtful," Christina agreed.

"Unbelievable," Ashley said.

Terence started the engine and pulled out of the parking lot. They weren't far down the road when Katie looked out the tinted gray windows and saw the two sisters stopped on the side of the road. A motorcycle stood beside their bikes and a tall, thin officer seemed to be speaking very seriously to the girls who wore chastened expressions.

"They're not wearing bike helmets," Ashley pointed out, looking over Katie's shoulder. "I bet that's why he stopped them."

"Know what else I bet?" Katie said, still watching as they drove away from the girls and the officer. "I bet his nameplate says—"

"Officer Winger," Ashley finished for her.

Katie nodded.

19

The limo stopped on the dirt driveway which led to Katie's house. "Bye, you guys. See you at school tomorrow," Katie said as she got out.

"Will you be all right there?" Ashley asked. "Is Mel back?"

"I don't know. But I'll be fine. Bye."

She stood and watched as the limo turned and drove away. Dizzy joined her, wagging his tail happily. "Hi, boy," she said, genuinely glad to see him.

Turning, she gazed at the house. It was still a bit dilapidated and the roof still sagged, but now it seemed friendly to Katie. It was home.

The side door creaked as she entered the cool kitchen. She yawned, suddenly realizing she was very tired. She checked Dizzy's dog food dish in the corner. There was food in it, so Mel had been around at some time.

On the kitchen table was a note in Mel's messy

writing. *Katie. I am at Mary Ellen's. When you come home from your friend's, give me a call at her house.* Katie was impressed. That showed more concern than she would have ever given him credit for.

She called Mary Ellen's and spoke to Mel. "I'll be home kind of late," he told her. "Maybe I'll see you."

"Okay," she said. "Want me to feed Dizzy?"

"Sure. Thanks."

Katie put fresh food in Dizzy's bowl. Then she checked Nagle's dish. The dried food she'd left was nearly gone. She replaced it with canned food and put out fresh water for both animals.

Upstairs, she found Nagle sleeping curled up in a ball on her bed. He lifted his small head and mewed at her, showing his spiky white teeth. Katie kicked off her boots as she scratched between his ears. "I didn't forget you," she assured him.

Katie's clothes were nearly dry, but uncomfortably stiff and dirty. She pulled them off and slipped into her blue flannel nightshirt.

Reaching under her bed, she pulled out her black-and-white covered notebook.

I've been away for two days, but it seems like longer. I'll miss Fern a lot, but maybe I'll see her again sometime. It's still hard to believe she was an angel, but she was. I'm learning that angels are mysterious. They come and go in unexpected ways. I hope I see her again, somehow, some way.

Katie rubbed her eyes. Being away from home for two nights had made her really tired. She stretched out on her bed and in moments was held fast by a deep, dreamless sleep.

When she next opened her eyes, the light of a blue-gray dawn filled her room. She sat up groggily, wondering why she'd awakened.

Something banged downstairs.

Katie's eyes went wide as she came fully awake. Who was in the house? Then she relaxed. It must be Mel just getting in. Her stomach grumbled in complaint and she remembered she hadn't eaten anything since before the picnic. Stretching, Katie swung her legs out of bed and headed downstairs to the kitchen.

When she reached the bottom of the stairs, she stopped short. "Aunt Rainie!" she exclaimed. "What are you doing home?"

Her aunt stood in front of her dressed in a long flowing, Hawaiian-print dress and a heavy fisherman-knit sweater. To Katie, it was an odd combination, but very lovable on Aunt Rainie. "Oh, Hawaii was just a bore, so we came back," she said, stretching her arms out to Katie. "Look at you. I am *so* glad to see you."

"Hawaii was *boring*?" Katie asked incredulously as Aunt Rainie wrapped her in a big, warm hug.

"It was pink," Uncle Jeff grumbled, lugging their large suitcase. "Way too pink. The colors were too bright there. They made your eyes hurt."

"The colors were too bright?" Katie repeated in

disbelief as Aunt Rainie finally loosened her tight hold. "I don't believe it. Is something wrong?"

"Oh, your aunt was worried about you," Uncle Jeff said.

"*I* was?" Aunt Rainie yelped. "*You* were the one always saying, 'I hope Katie's all right.'"

"You were the one said we had to come home," Uncle Jeff argued.

"Because you were driving me crazy. 'Katie is going to be lonely.' 'Katie's too young to be left alone.'"

"Well, you know Mel isn't exactly Mr. Reliable," Uncle Jeff grumbled. "And Katie *is* young."

"Oh, it doesn't matter," Aunt Rainie said with a wave of her hand. "We both wanted to come home. We didn't feel right being there without you. We missed you something fierce."

"Everything all right?" Uncle Jeff asked.

"Fine," Katie said. She looked into his blue-gray eyes and saw his concern for her. She went to him and hugged him hard. "I'm glad to see you," she said.

To her surprise, Uncle Jeff held her so tightly it almost hurt her ribs. She didn't mind, though. It felt good. "Glad to see you, too, girlie-girl," he said roughly. She knew he meant it.

After a moment he let her go and looked at her. "Don't you have school tomorrow?"

"Yep."

"Well, then get to bed!" he said with a smile as he began to climb the stairs. "You must be tired. I know I am."

Forgetting her hunger, Katie realized she *was* sleepy and turned to head back to bed.

"Wait, wait," Aunt Rainie said, digging in her large pocketbook. "I want to show you what I brought you." She pulled out something about the size of a baseball wrapped in tissue paper. "Here," she said presenting it to Katie.

Katie unwrapped the tissue, revealing the gift inside. Two hand-carved wooden foxes sat side by side, each wearing a delicately carved Hawaiian lei. Katie could hardly believe her eyes. "Why did you get me this?"

Aunt Rainie frowned. "Don't you like it?"

"I love it," Katie said truthfully. "I was just wondering why you thought of me when—"

"Really, it was the strangest thing," Aunt Rainie cut her off. "Jeff and I were walking down this dreamy white sand beach yesterday when I saw this man sitting under a palm tree, carving something. I just walked up to him to see what he was doing and he was carving this. I admired it and he held it up to me and said, 'Someone you love is waiting for this.' Isn't that odd?"

Katie nodded thoughtfully.

"Somehow I just thought of you right away," Aunt Rainie continued. "I wanted to pay him, but the man wouldn't take a dime. I insisted until he agreed, but he didn't have change for a twenty, so I went to get it from Jeff who was just a little ways off down the beach. When I turned back around, the man was gone and I was there holding these foxes. Can you imagine?"

"Did you ever see him again?" Katie asked.

"No," Aunt Rainie said. "But I never will forget him. He was Hawaiian and very fat. Aside from the fatness, there was nothing remarkable about him except his face. It wasn't his face so much, but his expression. It was so peaceful and happy. It was a face like . . . like . . ."

"Like an angel?" Katie asked.

Aunt Rainie's eyes went wide. "Yes! How did you know?"

"I just had a feeling," Katie said, hugging her aunt. "Thank you, Aunt Rainie. I love these foxes. They're really special."

"You're welcome, sweetie. Now Jeff's right. You really ought to get some more sleep."

Katie was on the third step when her aunt called her. "Where did this come from, hon?" she asked. In her hand was the blue, white, and pink woven blanket Katie had found draped over Fern.

"I . . . I found it, but . . . uh," Katie stammered, too surprised to think clearly. "Where was it?"

"Right here on the couch. I made this blanket for you when you were a baby," Aunt Rainie said, fondly smoothing it over her arm. "I was taking a weaving class at adult education at that time. Where did you find it?"

"Uh, it just sort of appeared the other day," Katie said. "I thought I'd lost it, though."

"No. It was right here." A faraway look came to Aunt Rainie's face. "Funny, when I agreed to be named as your guardian in your parents' will, I never thought I'd be called on to do it. Sad as it is, your parents dying so tragically, I sometimes feel it was a blessing having you come to us."

"You do?" Katie asked, her heart exploding with joy at these kind words.

"Yes, you've brought life and energy into the house. Jeff feels that way, too, though he has a hard time showing it," Aunt Rainie said. "He fretted about you the whole time we were away. You should have seen him!" Aunt Rainie gazed tenderly at the blanket. "I made this blanket for a little stranger. And now here you are, our own wonderful Katie-girl to love for always."

Katie ran to her aunt and hugged her one more time. "I love you," she said.

"I love you, too, honey," Aunt Rainie said, smoothing Katie's hair. Katie held on tight, then let go and smiled at her aunt.

"Well, you'd better get some sleep," Aunt Rainie said, smiling gently back at her.

"Good-night," Katie said, climbing the stairs. When she got to her room, it was awash with the first soft, golden-pink light of sunrise. She went to her window and gazed out.

So Aunt Rainie had woven that blanket. And somehow her parents had gotten it to her.

Fat pink clouds drifted into view. The rising sun rimmed them with a delicate gold outline.

"Mom, Dad," Katie spoke to the sunrise. "I know

you're out there. In some way you're watching me. I know that for sure now. Thanks for sending me here. I think I'm going to be all right. I still miss you—and I always will. But I'll also always cherish the happy memories—and I'm going to be *fine*."

She shut her eyes and leaned her head against the windowsill. She recalled the words in Christina's I Ching book. "Heaven and earth nourish all things."

Katie opened her eyes. The sun now blazed behind the clouds, sending bold rays of light shooting out from behind them. She looked hard, half expecting to see angels flying out of the magnificent clouds.

None appeared, but Katie felt certain they were all around her. Watching her. Guiding her. They'd been with her in the past and she hadn't even realized it, like when the woman came down the fire escape to speak to her.

And they would be there with her in the future. They would be there forever.

FOREVER ANGELS

by Suzanne Weyn

Everyone needs a special angel

Katie's Angel

0-8167-3614-6 $3.25 U.S./$4.50 Can.

Ashley's Lost Angel

0-8167-3613-8 $3.25 U.S./$4.50 Can.

Christina's Dancing Angel

0-8167-3688-X $3.25 U.S./$4.50 Can.

The Baby Angel

0-8167-3915-3 $3.25 U.S./$4.50 Can.

An Angel for Molly

0-8167-3912-9 $3.50 U.S./$4.95 Can.

The Blossom Angel

0-8167-3916-1 $3.50 U.S./$4.95 Can.

Available wherever you buy books.

Rainbow Bridge®

FOREVER ANGELS

AN ANGEL FOR MOLLY

by Suzanne Weyn

This little rich girl has everything— except what she really wants the most

Molly is thrilled. Her father has decided to let her join him on a business trip, and they'll be staying in an ancient Irish castle. She's hoping she can use the extra time with her father to talk about some things that are really important to her. Once they arrive in Ireland, though, Molly's father is distant and preoccupied. So Molly comes up with a reckless plan to get his attention. But when the plan backfires horribly, who can save Molly—and help her find her heart's desire?

0-8167-3912-9
$3.50 U.S. / $4.95 Can.

Available wherever you buy books.

A Special Preview

of

An Angel for Molly

The next morning, Molly's eyes snapped open abruptly. Loud, excited voices rose up from the courtyard below the window.

"They've brought Lucky Feather back!" Christina announced, standing by the window. "I see him! Right down there!"

"Lucky Feather!" Molly cried, leaping from the bed. "I thought they were keeping him in Connemare." Rushing to the window, she looked down at the regal, gleaming black stallion galloping in a circle with Alice on his back. Mr. and Mrs. Kingsley and Mr. Morgan stood nearby, studying Lucky Feather intensely.

Pulling her suitcase out from under the bed, Molly grabbed jeans and a sweatshirt and quickly dressed. "Wait for us," Ashley called as Molly hurried out the door, her long unbrushed hair flying loosely around her shoulders.

"I'll meet you down there," Molly called back to her. She ran down the twisting hallways, down the wide stone steps and through the dining room and study out to the courtyard. Mrs. Kingsley spotted her first and smiled. "He's a beauty, isn't he? You should have seen him run yesterday. He flew."

Molly shielded her eyes from the morning sun and studied the glistening stallion. He *was* a beauty. Majestic. Proud and strong. Of all the horses she had ever seen, Lucky Feather was the most magnificent. He was perfect.

Alice brought Lucky Feather to a halt in front of Molly. Gingerly, Molly smoothed her hand along his glossy coat. "He's gorgeous," she sighed. Something about the horse was truly inspiring to her. Lucky Feather awed her and made her heart quicken. It had to be his beauty—his astounding, perfect beauty. "Can I ride him, Dad?"

Mr. Morgan's brows furrowed in incredulous

disbelief. "I should say not! This is a champion racehorse. It's not a toy."

"But you know I can ride," Molly insisted.

Mr. Morgan waved her away dismissively. "Molly, please. I can't have this horse mis-handled. It's too large an investment."

"*He's* too large an investment," Molly corrected sullenly, annoyed at the way her father referred to this amazing creature as *it*. "He's not an it."

"Molly, don't act the spoiled brat, please," Mr. Morgan snapped. "I don't have the time for it right now."

He turned to Mr. Kingsley and began talking about the horse in a low, businesslike voice. Molly knew she'd been dismissed.

An angry sob choked its way into Molly's throat. She fought it down until only a petulant huff came out her mouth. Mr. Morgan didn't notice. He wasn't even paying attention to her anymore. She might as well have vanished for all he knew, she thought.

Molly felt a burning on her cheeks as if her father's rejecting words had hit her like an actual, physical slap. She bit on her lip to fight down tears. Was she being a spoiled brat, insisting on riding? No. It wasn't only that which hurt her feelings. It was that he didn't think she could do it. Wouldn't even consider the possibility that she could.

And why did he have to talk to her like that, so rudely, as if her feelings didn't matter, like she was some sort of pest? He made her feel so small—and in front of everyone, too!

Molly caught Alice's eye. Alice seemed to be studying her with pity in her eyes. Embarrassed, Molly smiled. "Why didn't you bring him to the farm in Connemare?" she asked.

"I don't know," Alice replied, tucking a strand of her blonde blunt-cut hair behind her ear. "Your father just changed his mind and decided he'd prefer him to stay here. There *is* an old stable down on the other side of this courtyard. The roof is down in one spot, but it can be boarded over and made usable."

"Cool," Molly said. "I'm glad he's here."

Alice nodded and sighed. "He's awfully beautiful. And fast!"

Mr. Kingsley took Lucky Feather and hitched him to the stone fence. "Let's go see what that stable really needs," he suggested to the Kingsley's and Alice. They walked off down a path that cut through the bare woods, leaving Molly alone with Lucky Feather.

The horse whinnied softly and swiveled his head back to gaze at Molly with deep black eyes. Molly stared at him, mesmerized. She felt a strong connection to this animal, as if his penetrating gaze was looking deep into her heart. Stroking his neck, she laid her cheek on his side.

Everyone was down at the stable. They'd be busy down there for a while. Who would ever know if she rode Lucky Feather right now? She knew she could do it.

With a quick glance down the path, Molly unhitched Lucky Feather. He was so tall she found it a little difficult to pull herself up onto the saddle. But once she did, a new sense of strength and wild freedom coursed through her. Clicking softly, Molly squeezed her knees into his sides to get him moving. He cantered smoothly at first. Then Molly leaned forward and let out the reins.

As if a tremendous wind had swept them up, Lucky Feather raced swiftly and smoothly around the courtyard. Handling him was almost effortless. Molly had never before felt so completely at ease in the saddle. She felt at one with the horse, moving together in a soaring, fluid motion.

From the corner of her eyes she saw Ashley, Katie, and Christina sitting on the stone fence watching her, looking very impressed. She felt proud and leaned further forward in the saddle, softly urging Lucky Feather to go faster. Was she showing off? Who cared? She felt wonderful. Lucky Feather heeded her silent command and ran even faster. He, too, seemed to exult in the pace and freedom of running. Molly imagined he was a winged unicorn about to soar into the air. If he had, she'd have hardly been surprised.

Molly had learned to jump a horse. Could Lucky Feather jump? Probably. This horse could do anything. Maybe he couldn't really leap into the air. Certainly, though, he could jump that two foot bench in the center of the courtyard. Molly had to find out how it would feel on Lucky Feather. It *had* to feel like flying.

Steering with the reins, she brought Lucky Feather to the farthest corner of the courtyard before turning him toward the bench in the center of the courtyard. She waved quickly to her friends and then raced toward the bench.

Molly lifted herself in the saddle getting into position to jump. They were nearly there, only a yard from the bench when a sound made her look up.

"Molly!" her father bellowed, his face red with rage. "Molly!" He stood at the entrance to the path, his fists balled at his side in fury.

Seized with panic, Molly pulled up tightly on the reins. With an angry whinny, Lucky Feather reared back and Molly felt the leather reins slip from her hands.

FOREVER ANGELS

KATIE'S ANGEL

by Suzanne Weyn

Katie thought she was all alone in the world . . .

When her parents died, Katie's world turned upside down. Forced to move in with uncaring relatives, she's never felt more alone. Katie can't stop missing her parents, and it seems she's always getting into trouble for one reason or another. Finally she can't take it any longer and decides to run away. And that's when Katie discovers that she's not as alone as she thinks she is. There's someone special looking out for her—someone she never would have guessed—who can help Katie find the happiness she's been missing.

0-8167-3614-6
$3.25 U.S. / $4.50 Can.

Available wherever you buy books.

Rainbow Bridge®

₣OREVER ₳NGELS

ASHLEY'S LOST ANGEL

by Suzanne Weyn

Ashley's searching for a miracle

Perfect Ashley's perfect life is suddenly falling apart. The boy she likes doesn't like her anymore, her grades are sinking, and her horse is sick. But that's nothing compared to her parents' problems. Their money troubles may force them to close their horse farm and give up the only home Ashley's ever known. Worst of all, they're even talking about getting a divorce. Ashley's desperate for an answer, something that can turn her life around. Is anyone listening?

0-8167-3613-8
$3.25 U.S. / $4.50 Can.

Available wherever you buy books.

FOREVER ANGELS
CHRISTINA'S DANCING ANGEL

by Suzanne Weyn

All she wants to do is dance . . . like an angel

Christina dreams of dancing on air, but reality keeps bringing her down to earth. Her dance teacher thinks Christina should give it up, that Christina will never have the right build for dancing. Christina thinks where there's a will there's a way. If she can only make herself over, she's sure her wishes will come true. Her friends liked the old Christina just fine, and they're worried she's trying too hard to change. Christina is truly more special than anyone can guess, least of all Christina, but it will take a special being to make her see the light.

0-8167-3688-X
$3.25 U.S. / $4.50 Can.

Available wherever you buy books.

Rainbow Bridge®